Let Me Tell You Everything

Memoirs of a Lovesick Intellectual

Let Me Tell You Everything

Memoirs of a Lovesick Intellectual

by Barbara Bottner

HARPER & ROW, PUBLISHERS, New York
Grand Rapids, Philadelphia, St. Louis, San Francisco,
London, Singapore, Sydney, Tokyo

Library of Congress Cataloging-in-Publication Data
Bottner, Barbara.
    Let me tell you everything : memoirs of a lovesick
intellectual / by Barbara Bottner.
        p.   cm.
    Summary: An articulate, intelligent teenager with strong
ideas about feminism faces a conflict when she falls in love
with her social studies teacher.
    ISBN 0-06-020596-2 : $
    ISBN 0-06-020597-0 (lib. bdg.) : $
    [1. High schools—Fiction. 2. Schools—Fiction.
3. Teachers—Fiction.] I. Title.
PZ7.B6586Le 1989   88-22066
[Fic]—dc19   CIP
                                                 AC

For my husband

A special thanks to
Ellen Rabinowich

Chapter One

Rosanna. You could scan every senior: the pretty dark-haired girls, the rich preppies, the bubbly cute freckled cheerleaders, the sleek high-grade-point-average prima donnas—at seventeen you had to be a real dog not to have something going for you—but when it came to Rosanna you had to throw out the old chart, trash it completely, and get a new one that had Madonna on it, or Cher, or Princess Di. One that was only for state-of-the-art beauties, and then you had to make room at the very top of it for Rosanna.

When boys looked at her you could see their metabolism change: Their skin would start to glow; they'd get clever, sweat, and become athletic all at once.

And she acted like she didn't even notice! I don't know how she pulled it off, even though I stared at her constantly, all through our advanced social studies class. She'd sit in the very front row as if she were about to give her opinions to the General Assembly of the United Nations.

We were about to study *The Greening of America.* For a minute I concentrated on the jacket cover. It said that the modern corporate state poisoned our values and that war, poverty, and depersonalization were the results. It was written years ago, during the hippie era. My mom was a hippie, so now I'd get to understand the way she thought. This book sounded pretty interesting, but then I got a waft of Rosanna's perfume, and my eyes drifted away from our national problems to the local one: Rosanna.

Sure I studied her. First of all, she had perfect skin. Creamy skin, the color of nut butter; warm liquidy skin, like somebody had just poured it over her. Rosanna Dakis. I didn't know what her background was, except that I wouldn't mind having it. Not if it meant I would get this gorgeous figure with big rounded breasts that bounced like they were made of pure happiness, a tiny waist, long legs, and those incredible kind of ankles, like Grace Kelly had in that movie classic *Rear Window.* Why should ankles, just a bone and a joint, be able to drive boys crazy? On Rosanna they did that. I guess it was those big brown eyes that looked at you like they'd never seen anything important before, that nice nose you could ski down if you were a Tom Thumb, and those lips and white teeth that Coppola would pay a million dollars to have in one of his films. God really had a good time when he made this girl. He probably went over her a bunch of times to get everything perfect. I don't believe even God could get her that right the first time.

Rosanna had two sisters, and she shared lots of clothes with them, so she was always well dressed. But frankly, a circus tent would have looked fine on her, and Betsy Ross's flag would have been ravishing. There was nothing that wouldn't have looked glorified resting on that girl's shoulders.

You got the picture by now.

Don't get me wrong. Me, Brogan, I'm no factory reject, and I don't generally spend my precious time writing rave reviews about other senior girls at Bellmont. I like my share of the attention, even more than my share, which you would understand if you knew more about my crazy family.

However, God didn't go over *my* blueprints three or four times. They showed me to Him, and He said: "Looks okay." And I am, but certainly if He'd taken a little more time He would have noticed that some joker went a little nutsy on the ears (and gave me large instead of medium). I guess they thought I was going to be a composer. And my ankles could have used a little whittling down; likewise, my fat fingers that no amount of long nails will ever hide. Still, I made out okay on the important points. I slid by with my mom's green eyes, and pretty good features. I'm just not a show stopper. My knees pucker and I have 113 freckles, size nine feet, and I'm only 5'4"! On the map between real bow-wow ugly and drop-dead-your-life-is-made gorgeous, I'm just middle of the road "cute."

Let me just say: I'm grateful. One look at Darlene Kuebler and I could almost get holy with gratitude. In her case,

God probably said: "Hey guys, you're getting the drift, do the next fifty on your own." And He jumped into the Heavenly Sauna. Then some joker must have said, "How would no chin look on a girl with short legs?" I'm glad I wasn't in that crop.

It was the start of second semester at Bellmont, Brooklyn's most archaic high school—it looked like the architect had snatched the design out of an old Archie Comics book. Inside, however, we had all the usual current problems—teenage pregnancy, drugs, suicide attempts, and divorce. Maybe in Archie and Veronica's day things were different. I hope so. That's when my parents were teenagers.

Anyway, Fettlestein would soon be marching in for our class, and her reputation preceded her: lots of homework and papers, and a state of emergency akin to a national alert. No problem. I liked social studies because it was like planetary gossip: how people and societies got the way they are, and how history contributes to the mess we're in.

Fettlestein's rep was also that she was very stimulating. Well, I hoped she was because I needed some stimulation in my life that didn't come from two parents treating each other like their living room was the Gaza Strip. I bet Israelis and Palestinians get along better than my parents, Buster and Nan Arthur.

I opened my brand-new notebook and wrote the only neat words that it would see the entire year: "Social Studies, Second Semester." After this my handwriting would degenerate into scribbles.

"Hey, Brogan!" That was Michelle. "I'm in love."

So what else is new?

"I'm concentrating," I said. "I'll talk to you in study hall."

Michelle was always in love. So was everyone else, except for a couple of types who were heading for ground-breaking careers in the CIA or the Mafia. Me, I was taking this semester off from the adrenaline. Gary, my last boyfriend, was superficial, remote, and wreaked havoc on my innards—I gained five pounds and started writing bad poetry. I was hung up over someone more immature than an amoeba. Gary didn't understand me or my family. Lucky for him, his parents were Mr. and Mrs. America; they were nice! In my house it was living hell. So Gary and I split up. He didn't like the way I sobbed in the movies when someone helped another person. Kindness broke me up so badly I would weep with awful and noisy gusto. Naturally, Gary thought I was nuts.

The major parts in *my* soap opera were Nan, Buster, and myself. Nan was struggling with conditional love—unconditional was something I hadn't seen since I had learned how to crawl. Buster, on the other hand, was a Black Belt in Conditional Love, which meant I either performed with my cute personality, terrific grades, and fabulous sense of humor, or I could count on getting my affection from the neighbor's dog Ryan. Which wasn't a bad idea, because dogs are suckers for affection, just like me.

But I did perform, all the time. I wanted my father to like me—sometimes I felt like my life depended on it. Then my mother would get mad and they'd fight. Lately it was getting pretty sticky. Sometimes I thought they were headed for Divorce City. And sometimes I thought I would offer to drive them. I wanted to be the one who said, "Look, we've got to sit down and talk. We're growing in different directions. We have to get a divorce."

I didn't have the guts to do that. But the tension had been escalating. I'd been arguing with Buster about capitalism, of all things. He'd built up a company, which built toasters and fans, from scratch. Recently it had merged with an international conglomerate and Buster had begun to travel all the time. He loved business, but he would sell fans to the Eskimos if he could and that bothered me. I argued about the markups, saying everyone should be able to afford a toaster. Sometimes he used cheap materials, and he also employed illegal aliens, whom he exploited. Buster said I didn't understand business. He was right. And he was rich. I thought we should all be doing home improvement on Planet Earth and I told him so.

"Easy for you to say." Buster glared. "You never had to earn a living."

"You mean a person can't do both?"

He'd shake his head sadly as if to say there were mysterious laws of life I was not able to understand. He'd grown up in the poorest streets of Brooklyn and had done everything by himself. His manufacturing company was a monument to his ambition and drive. He was a fighter and he wanted me, his only child, to be a fighter too. I wasn't against fighting—I just wanted to be sure what I was fighting for. Since I hadn't grown up on the streets, fighting for big bucks was no more real to me than fighting over religion or tribal territories.

So Buster thought I had New Age fairy dust between my ears, not reality, and certainly not the brand of reality he had in mind.

"You'll see," he'd predict.

I'd see I was wrong, he meant.

I was more like my mother: pro women's rights; saving whales, political prisoners, and national coastlines; passionately against apartheid and nuclear escalation. I hoped this semester with Fettlestein would inform me so that I could give Buster a real hard time, and spit out facts and statistics until he would have to change his mind.

I guess I also thought that if I were a knockout like Rosanna, my father would listen to my point of view. I got the impression that though he worshiped beautiful women, he didn't like women as people. In his mind, beauties were something else: goddesses.

Rosanna would have known what to do. She would have had my father wrapped around her little finger. She'd smile one of those port-in-a-storm smiles, and Buster the Combustible would melt like an M & M on a radiator.

The bell rang. Now Fettlestein would march in on her Red Cross one-inch-heel brown shoes with the fraying tassels, open *The Greening of America*, and get down to business, and I would have to end this subconscious aria of sincere but aimless worry, and bring my intelligence into the act. I would have to answer questions about America's lack of community and its alienation, and decide if the sixties and seventies created a revolution in consciousness or just a hazy dream.

This was fine with me, just as long as there weren't any numbers. Numbers made my vision blurry, except on price tags. I can remember the price of everything I've ever bought, including the tax. Sometimes when I'm bored I add myself up.

"Brogan!" Michelle leaned over, about to broadcast the latest information about the state of her love affair with Art Boyleton, as Fettlestein opened the door. Quickly I flipped open my looseleaf and looked up. Amazing! Over winter vacation Fettlestein had turned into a man!

I wasn't that surprised; she'd always walked funny.

On second look, however, it wasn't Fettlestein. It was the most gorgeous man over thirty to walk the streets of this town. Rowland Price! He was saying how he'd gotten reassigned. Fettlestein was not going to work this term for personal reasons.

"We are going to decide in this room if America is on the right track or not." He smiled. "Important question, don't you think? One I really care about."

Do you understand? The William Hurt of Bellmont was standing in front of my social studies class. He was so serious, so intense. Just my type. I would become a scholar, to thank God for realizing the importance of heartthrobs in education.

The way I felt now was the way the boys must feel when they looked at Rosanna. My skin tingled, I wanted to sing.

Mr. Price was discussing assignments. The first was an interview with someone whose life was affected by one of the issues discussed in Chapter One.

I raised my hand. "Is a dot matrix printer acceptable for assignments?" I asked. Bogus question. I didn't own a computer.

Price nodded. "You bet."

Maybe cute would be enough for him. Maybe when he realized how deep I was, how provocative, how tortured my homelife was, that would be all he needed to take an interest in me. His big brown eyes stayed on me for a minute. Oh God. Maybe Mr. Price and I knew each other in a past life that had nothing to do with Brooklyn or second semester of senior year. And maybe we would come to recognize a Great Bond. As for me, I already recognized it.

I looked at Michelle to see if she was having the same reaction as me. Apparently not. She was drawing a picture of Art's hair. Personally I preferred guys who didn't blow dry their locks. Mr. Price's hair was curly and sandy colored and naturally fell into layers on his broad and handsome head. He had wide shoulders and an incredibly clean-cut and honest face that was too beautiful for my heart. How could I learn anything from him?

Good-bye Fettlestein, hello life!

He was writing on the greenboard. Then someone yawned and stretched in a gradual and sensuous unfolding of various ideal body parts. I looked up. It was Rosanna. Price also turned to look. And his face told me: I was such a jerk. I could forget about Mr. Price. I could bring him

9

trays of homemade chocolate brownies, brilliant theories on the CIA, tickets for a cruise to Hawaii, winning lottery numbers. He would never notice.

Not as long as Rosanna could yawn.

Chapter Two

Drat! Maybe I couldn't stretch like a Playmate of the Month, but I had great ideas. And Price would know about them soon. For the whole semester we'd be reading *The Greening of America*. Fine! I already had theories from studying my parents. From careful observation of these two people, I could basically see how all of society worked.

I loved my own mind. When Nan and Buster were at it, I'd shut the door and try to ponder the larger questions. I suppose you could say I had a Large Question Mania. I never liked details. My idea of heaven would be to corner Freud, Marx, Jesus, and Einstein and force them to explain the world to me. This type of thing got on my parents' nerves, but since they appreciated that I wasn't into drugs they put up with it.

Anyway, I figured I had to knock Price's eyes out with my interview of my mom and dad. Through what they said, I could illustrate Reich's theory about why our country was in deep trouble. Reich said it was due to impoverishment of the spirit, lack of compassion, and loss of the creative impulse. From the vantage point of my family, I had to agree.

While my mother tossed the salad, and my father opened the liquor cabinet, I launched into a speech about the perversions, failures, and lack of responsibility that threatened America.

"This teacher doesn't sound constructive," my father said, pouring the first of his many drinks of the evening. He usually had a couple of vodkas before dinner, a watered-down one during dinner, and then he'd move on to beer while he watched T.V. in the family room. Before he started chug-a-lugging alcohol, my father was really athletic-looking, with a big chest and arms and a thick neck. Now his chin was getting fleshy and he had a big belly to match.

"It's constructive to look around you and see the problems a society is having," I said, dishing out the veggies in our homespun kitchen. Mom had put lots of baskets and dishes on the wall, and to look at it, you'd think this were the house the three bears lived in—it was inviting, warm, and natural.

"Brogan has a point," said my mother. "The system is distorted and so are we."

"Maybe you are," said Buster, "but I'm just fine. Now please pass the potatoes. I'm hungry."

"What do you mean, Mom?"

"Take my own case."

"Oh *no!*" said my dad. "It wasn't the damn *system* that made you drop out. You were scared."

"It was the system that scared me!"

"Your mother didn't want to face the world, so she married me. Now she feels she missed out on something." My father gulped down the last of his drink. "She did! She missed working fourteen-hour days, riding crowded subways, dealing with neurotic bosses, and trying to outguess the market."

"I know I could have done more," mumbled Nan, "with support." She ran a finger through her dark hair that fell in front of her strong, elegant face so often, sometimes I really thought she was hiding behind it. Nan had beautiful eyes, greenish grayish, fringed with naturally dark lashes. She didn't even need to wear eye makeup, but sometimes she needed blusher because her face would get pale-looking from her being so unhappy.

"Support? I gave you support for your pottery wheel downstairs that cost a pretty penny and you hardly ever use it."

"I *do* use it . . . to relax," said Nan.

"Support!" My father was on his way to getting drunk. "Where's this mysterious support suposed to *come* from?" he boomed. Liquor always made him sound like stereo.

"From the people who love you," said my mother, picking at her food.

"Let me tell you about the support *I* got. What I got was

a father who kicked me out of the house when I turned seventeen. So I built a company. Myself. And here I am. Here we *all* are."

"And the rest is world history," said Nan.

"Look, Dad, men at least expect they'll have to function in the world. In Mom's day women weren't sure."

"And in your day, Brogan?"

"Well, my generation learned from Mom's. At least we're not programmed to be cowards."

"Well, I hope your generation and you will be happier than your mom is," Buster said.

"Well, *you* sure didn't make me happy," said Nan.

"I'm not *supposed* to make you happy! Anyway, you don't *want* to be happy. You think it's intellectually superior to be miserable!" Buster poured another drink.

It was true—when you look at my mother, the word "happy" would not zing into your mind.

"This was supposed to be a discussion," I said. "For school, remember?"

"Well, you're always looking to fight with me, isn't that true, you two?" Buster, a big man, jerked up from the table. Now his force field was dangerously enlarged. "Somewhere along the line I did something wrong and damn if I know what it is!"

I waited until he was gone. Maybe now Nan and I could communicate. "So Ma, if your life had been different, how do you think it might have been?"

"Brogan, not now, please." She picked up some plates and went into the kitchen.

I went back to the dining room and ate cold capitalistic roast beef and potatoes by myself. Why didn't Nan want to discuss this with me? I was on her side. Women have been losers and victims for so long. *I understood.* I could help her if she'd let me.

"You don't know what you're talking about," said my father later as he watched a basketball game on the tube. "Things don't really change, no matter how many books are written. This teacher sounds like he has a chip on his shoulder."

"His shoulders are just fine; so's his brain. He just wants us to think about things."

"Sometimes you can get yourself into a stew by thinking too much," he said.

I didn't say you can get stewed faster by drinking.

When I was done with my homework I took a long hot shower, the kind you wish could change your whole life just from the sheer heat and force of the water. I stayed under a long, long time. I always tried to melt in the shower, melt into a younger, happier me. Sometimes it worked, and I went back to the time my parents cuddled and laughed at each other's jokes instead of snarling at each other. When I got out I dried my hair and put oils on all over my skin. My legs were long and pretty. My torso was firm. My long, brown hair shimmered on my skull. Now my green eyes appeared larger and my skin steamed. I didn't worry about my ankles and could temporarily subscribe to the theory that I was gorgeous. In this tiny vaporized chamber I wondered what it would be like lying next to Mr. Price. Was he all hairy and muscular? Did he have a belly? And those arms . . .

I dried my hair and wished. Oh, Rowland, I would say. He would smile and listen to my theories. He would see how perceptive I was about the world. He wouldn't be like Buster, set in his ideas, righteous and wrong at the same time. No, Mr. Price would be curious about what I had to say and worried about the right things. And I would understand him like nobody ever had. We would read and think together and reach *Guinness Book of World Records* levels of communication. Then he would not be able to do anything except kiss me all over even if he had hundreds of school reports to read. He'd throw them across the room and make me a woman.

The next day in class he was so dramatic. "America is dealing death." He snapped us out of our private thoughts by reading the first sentence of the book.

"Pretty strong statement! It was written sixteen years ago when you kids were just After Dinner Mints. Now we can examine exactly what has changed in this country since you were born."

What a brilliant thinker! Did everyone realize how brilliant he was? Did his wife? (Was he married?) Did she get to set the table with him every night? What was she like? Was she smart like him or adoring like me? Or was he single, lonely, but devoted to his work? Perhaps he was dating, searching for his soul mate but not finding her.

Suddenly Michelle gasped. Her eyes popped out and her hand went over her heart. I followed her awestruck gaze to Rosanna, who was wearing a V-neck sweater that revealed astonishing cleavage. Rosanna's cleavage was no longer a mystery to anyone, least of all Rowland Price, whose desk she faced. Her elbows were on her desk and her whole body was leaning forward, her big eyes searching his for a larger truth—at least that's what the expression she wore seemed to say. Mr. Price studied Rosanna, happy, no doubt, to oblige her with this truth all right. It was a tidy little scene: student, teacher, and cleavage.

I didn't let my reaction show. I couldn't compete with the cleavage, the thick, wavy hair—I just wasn't built for Miss America contests. So the question was, How could I deaden my heart? How could I make it stop banging around in my chest like a pipe bomb about to explode? There was only Mr. Price and myself in my world, but somehow Rosanna was snatching him away. My world was doomed.

Finally Rosanna took out the barrettes holding her hair in a knot and shook her mane free. It cascaded down her back as if in slow motion. I could have sworn I saw Mr. Price's eyes spin like a wheel of fortune.

"Okay, class," said Price. "Who wants to comment on the premise of the first chapter?"

Mr. Price looked at me but I wasn't going to help him out. Let him get gorgeous Rosanna's fascinating opinions. His eyes settled on Ira Moss. Ira wore all junk-store clothes, but he had a fifty-dollar haircut complete with blue streak.

He wore a small earring. He wasn't gay, just a New Age fashion plate.

"He says technology is out of control," said Ira.

"What he says is that due to technology we've lost our real selves," said Michelle, who glanced over at Art for his approval.

Now Rosanna raised her hand. Perhaps she would be stupid. Oh, make my day, Rosanna, make my day.

"I agree with Reich's premise," she said with impeccable dignity. "He says we've lost our uniqueness so we can fit in the system." She batted her lashes to assure Price that *she* hadn't lost anything. He got it too, because his face gave out beams of approval, beams and beams of glowing energy. Beams, if you ask me, of love.

"We're playing bumper cars with the global ecology. We have egos that need tune-ups every hour," I spit out.

"Reich was a malcontent who overreacted to the hippies and thought all of society was going to change." Susan Seymour spoke with an edge in her voice that would have cut glass. "And he's overcritical of America. Maybe you would rather be in China." She glared at me. "You can't be lonely when you take a lunch break with two thousand workers. But they're all nobodies, puppets of the state."

"We're all nobodies here!" Bruce Tailor had one of those faces that lit up when he spoke. He wore a faded shirt and jeans and had silky brown hair. "In China at least they take care of your medical problems."

"Hey, it's only a *book*, man! You don't have to think

about it except in this class." Ira stretched his long legs into the aisle.

"*Wrong!*" said Bruce. "Did you know our government knew about asbestos poisoning twenty years ago and did nothing to protect workers?"

"That's not in the first chapter," said Susan.

"Neither is the fact that my uncle . . . oh never mind."

"Don't stop now," said Ira sarcastically, "or we won't sleep tonight."

Bruce gritted his teeth and said, "My uncle is dying of asbestos poisoning."

"Look," Susan rushed in, "I'm sorry about your uncle, Bruce, but we have a great government. We cure horrible diseases, we take in refugees, and we have freedom." And then she popped out of her seat.

"That's why we have so many mass murderers," said Bruce.

"Susan, sit down, please." Mr. Price's eyes were cloudy. The blue changed and his jaws clenched like some actors do it in the movies. Was it possible? He was even more handsome!

"Yeah well, we build missiles, poor people are worse off than ever, and our crime rate could give you a heart attack—other than that we have a great government." I turned around and saw Bruce Tailor was livid. I liked passion in a person.

Susan headed for the door. "I'm exercising my spontaneity and originality, which Reich thinks are *so* missing in modern man," she said, and she was history.

"Amazing," said Mr. Price. "Without any territory, religion, or armies, we've had disorder, the number-one topic in the chapter."

"But there *is* an army," I said. "In our minds. We came in with ideas, and ideas are what make war."

"Excellent!" Mr. Price jumped up, and a shock of hair fell over one eye. He gave me a steady dose of the A-1 wear-tested best smile in America. I shivered. Then a warm glow covered me, and I was sweating like I had just taken a stroll down the equator. And then I had to wonder, was that smile as good as the one he gave Rosanna? Or was hers juicier? Did it last longer, and were the rays warmer when they went to her? The only way to know was to try to make him smile at me again.

But what was I doing getting so carried away? I believed in feminism, which said women had to be independent, strong, self-reliant. I had this idea that feminists controlled their emotions, that they didn't have body juices like mine that favored torchy, yearning, Aretha Franklin kind of love. It was wrong, these feelings of wanting to throw myself at Mr. Price's feet—opposite to self-possession, self-determination, and self-respect. Worse yet, it was servile to want Mr. Price to be my god.

I knew better. Where did these feelings come from, anyway? Were they normal or sick? Normal was wanting Peter Druz to notice you at basketball practice and maybe call you that night and make bad jokes you would probably laugh at. That was bad enough, because smart girls like me should be doing our own thing—studying a language (*n'est-*

ce pas?) or competitive swimming, or playing the piano.

I should have been thinking about getting into college and what I'd study there, but no, all I wanted was to grow bigger breasts for Mr. Price. Or buy violet contact lenses, or memorize *The Greening of America*. That's how strong my conditioning was.

The bell rang. I swished past Price's desk hoping he'd catch my dab of Paris and fall into obsessive love with me. My body was winning over my mind again and it wasn't even a close match.

Ira walked by me. "My ego doesn't need a tune-up," he said. "I just had a three-thousand-mile check-up."

"Get your money back," said Bruce Tailor, and he winked at me. By now everyone was swiftly on their feet, and I was swept out the door squished between the guys, but I snuck a look back.

Rosanna was only just beginning to pick up her books. Those connecting sincere eyes of Mr. Price's that could pull you wherever they wanted were fixed on her face, and this time he wasn't smiling at all.

Was I imagining things? No, I saw it: that serious look that could burn you, scorch you; it was gamma ray voltage, particles sprayed all over, subatomic neutrons bouncing off the wall. And the worst part of it was that even though it wasn't meant for me, I was singed by its heat.

Gloria Steinem, Bella Abzug, Simone de Beauvoir— *help!!!*

Chapter Three

Dripping in rhinestones and denim, Michelle was sprawled out on my bed tearing pages out of *Mademoiselle* and squealing with dangerously high levels of enthusiasm. I tried to ignore her with equal levels of scholarship.

"Don't you love *backless*? I mean, love *is* the word, isn't it? And isn't mauve divine? On *me*, I mean?"

"Uh-huh."

"Don't 'uh-huh' me, you haven't even looked up. I am appealing to your female genes."

I was reading *The Greening of America*, trying to understand Reich's position on the New Deal and President Roosevelt's legislation that attempted to promote economic recovery and social reform after the Depression. Reich's book traced America's present problems from the past.

"Brogan! My birthday party is in two and a half weeks.

It's my Sexy Seventeen." She leaped up on the bed, and let herself fall down again. "We're in our prime and we must look gorgeous." She made it sound like a national imperative like lower grain prices or federally sponsored mortgage loans. *"Gorgeous!"*

"Parties! Little vacations from technological imprisonment. Do you realize the New Deal failed to reform capitalism because consciousness can't be legislated?" I looked at Michelle's dumbstruck face. "No, you didn't realize that, did you?"

"What I didn't realize was that you are avoiding the subject of dating. All this political concern is just a cover. Anyway, what do you want me to do, raise consciousness over hors d'oeuvres? We're teenagers, dammit. With weight problems and tests! Lighten up."

"I was born heavy."

"Well, put down the New Deal—you'll feel lighter. Look at this dress. It would look perfect on you."

What I thought would look good on me was Appalachian children finally getting fed. She threw the magazine at me, and I caught it.

"So? Drop-dead strapless, or virginal with a high neck?"

"Michelle, these dresses cost ninety bucks! Did you know you could feed an entire family in the Philippines for three months for sixty-six dollars? In Haiti you can buy a goat for five dollars."

"Only misfits who are terrified of boys know facts like that."

I tuned out for a minute and pictured myself in one of the low-cut numbers with big puffy sleeves. Maybe a push-up bra would achieve what nature hadn't. Then I mentally added lots of feathery hair and mascara. That would do it! Do what? Do everything society said to do in order to land a guy. Just more conditioning! But what was one little night of glamour going to do to the world? Nothing, right? So before she left I promised to buy a new dress. Michelle figured she would go vampy and I'd go sweet, and we'd have Spring Evening Wear Look covered.

Satisfied that my appearance would live up to her expectations, Michelle finally left and I got back to Chapter Three, which was two weeks ahead of what we were reading in class. The book was almost four hundred pages and I wanted to finish it before anyone else.

That night, I read over one of those ads that says how poor Miguel's family lives on five dollars a month and I got sick. I wondered what Mr. Price would think about my problem. Would he remind me that I was old enough to start thinking for myself?

Anyway, I had no one to go to Michelle's party with.

I got back to my homework. Why did I love theories so much? I did, though. I loved theories more than life. Theories were pure, so they could be perfect. Theories were better than people, except special people. Rare people. Only the most refined and exceptional person could be as inspiring as a theory. I wasn't mentioning any names.

Buster had this terrible habit: When he wanted to come into my room, he knocked and entered simultaneously, which obliterated the reason for the knock in the first place.

But I couldn't go through my usual objections with him tonight. He hadn't had a drink at supper, and I didn't want him to start slugging vodkas now.

Uninvited, he came in and sat on my bed.

"Europe," he said. "Your dad is going to Europe for a week. What do you think of that?" He said it as if it took a special kind of person to go overseas for only a week. "They know how to live, those people."

"Which people?"

"The Italians, the French. They know how to enjoy life, know what I mean?" The glint in his eye should have warned me.

"You mean they like to sit in cafes, and they have more parks in their cities than we do." I knew this from the movies.

"No, I mean they know how to *live*. To have a good time."

"Americans like to have a good time." I said. I was thinking of Michelle's party. It was no use asking my father what he thought. He would only question me why I was worrying about Third World people instead of worrying about getting a date. "Americans are pleasure addicts."

"It's unnerving," he said. "I have the entire moral conscience of a nation using my toothpaste."

I decided to keep my mouth shut about the failure of the New Deal to really reform business in this country. He'd flip!

"Anyway, I mean European men. *They* know how to keep their wives happy and still have a good time." Buster's skin suddenly seemed to grow moist. His eyes squinted and his mouth twisted.

"Well, how do they treat their daughters?"

"They adore them. And the daughters *respect* their fathers. See, men think about things differently there." Buster settled down into my chair. And he winked at me. "They have a healthy attitude. Not like us; we have such a narrow view of marriage."

I wasn't crazy about the gist of the conversation, and he'd only disagree with my point of view anyway. But I couldn't help myself. "The whole world basically believes the same thing: women are supposed to serve men, give up their own lives, and love every minute of it." I wanted to say, *"Don't tell me about your creepy ideas of marriage. It hurts. This isn't good for me."* Instead I said, "We have the highest divorce rate in the whole world."

"And do you know why?" He was rolling now. "I'll tell you why. Because in Europe they figured out how to make marriages last! Mistresses! So men don't have to leave their wives and families." Buster announced this with a great sense of personal satisfaction.

Once I would have felt terribly pleased that my father was confiding in me. Now I felt like I was covered with grease.

"So you're going to Europe to get a mistress?" I said, trying to sound sophisticated.

"It's a pretty good system. Maybe if Americans thought that way we'd have a lower divorce rate. Tell *that* to your brilliant social studies teacher!"

"And you think that's the right thing to do?"

"Look, I'm human."

"What does *that* mean?"

"It means I do the best I can, which ain't always that good. What do you want from Europe?"

Perfume.

Perfume that will drive Mr. Price crazy, make him riveted to me, make him forget Rosanna. But suddenly I wished my father would just go fix himself a drink and leave me out of his sick fantasies.

"Let's just forget this little talk, anyway." He was bursting his buttons, I guess from unloading his lousy secret life on me. "So what do you want?"

"I don't want anything."

"What a strange girl," said my father. "I want to buy you presents and you won't let me."

The next morning, I dressed for school carefully. I put on eye shadow that matched my green jumpsuit, which I knew showed off my figure. I put my hair in a high ponytail. I stared in the mirror and couldn't deny the result. I was sassy, and my long legs and small waist were definitely okay. I snuck into my mom's room, and dabbed on Opium. Well, I bet even Mrs. Gandhi wore perfume, and Margaret Thatcher too.

"Finally!" said Michelle when we got to school. "Who is the lucky guy? John Adair? Peter Druz?"

"Down, girl. I just repossessed my green eye shadow from the bottom of my old Nikes." We sat down next to each other.

"Art says you can invite his brother to my party."

"Art also says the most important thing in life is the Mets." I opened up my looseleaf to give my comment zing.

"Art is deeper than *I* am," said Michelle. "Anyway, what's wrong with baseball?"

"Nothing. When all the people on the planet have had a good meal, all 5.3 billion of them should sit down together and watch a game."

"You're getting worse. Not to mention you happen to love spiking a volleyball yourself, *n'est-ce pas?*" Michelle took out her brush and madly started to fix her hair.

"If the world was ending tomorrow, you would listen to me."

"If the world was ending tomorrow, I'd be fooling around with Art starting now. Look, just act normal at my party, okay, and I'll try to get you admitted into shock therapy." And she opened up her own book for punctuation.

After Price's class, I hung around until everyone left. Including Rosanna, whose waist, it was now apparent, was the size of a small rubber band. She was wearing a cinch belt, and the rest of her body was throbbing above and below it. While Michelle was reading *Mademoiselle*, Rosanna had been having private coaching sessions with Hugh Hefner. Finally, Rosanna was gone. I made my move.

"Brogan." Mr. Price looked at me and smiled, but it wasn't warm and personal; it was his polite, professionally charming smile. "How's the work coming along?" He was at his desk sorting papers.

"This isn't about work." It's about that I love you. "I have a moral question."

"Shoot."

"It's about parties. They're everything Reich says they are—alienated ego trips. In his chapter about the New Deal, he talks about our national tendency to crass materialism. I don't want to be part of that. Do you see what I mean?"

He didn't answer my question, but at least he stopped moving around the stuff on his desk. "I'm impressed that you're up to Chapter Three! Well, do you agree with Reich's assessment of the New Deal?"

"Oh yes!" I said eagerly. "Individual power got redirected to labor unions, but unfortunately it didn't really alter the basic impotence of the people."

"So you feel that it failed?"

"Absolutely!" Drat! I hadn't finished the chapter, and I was getting in over my head. "Don't you?"

"No, actually. Brogan, I think improvement comes in stages." Now he came around and sat on his desk. "More was accomplished in the New Deal than Reich admits. I believe that the unfortunate events with the House Committee on Un-American Activities actually gave birth to a *backlash* that strengthened our commitment to democracy."

"Reich says it didn't."

"It gave the working man a forum: a union."

"I'll have to read it again."

I didn't understand enough to argue, and worse, *we disagreed!*

"I suggest you do. After all, if you find yourself in whole-sale agreement with this book, you'll be commiting the crime Reich finds the most egregious—giving up your own autonomy!" Mr. Price stood up and started to pace. "Let me ask you, Brogan, what do you want from your life?"

"I don't know, Mr. Price. I guess I don't want it to get worse."

"That's an odd answer. Why should it?"

"Because of the world."

"Is the world the reason it will get worse? Is that what you mean?"

"No." But I couldn't tell him what I meant now; it was too late. When I was a kid I saw the world differently. The air felt so good on my skin, and being alive itself seemed like such an advantage. There was some idea of goodness, of natural happiness.

"You would like the world to be different?"

"Yes!" I said, almost shouting.

He nodded. "Yes . . ." he said almost sadly.

"But . . ." Oh, God, I was getting choked up. The world had been magical. Going for walks, floating in rowboats, the nights when my mom played the piano, the mornings when I woke up with hope in my chest. Excitment, *life*—something in me cried those mornings—*life to be lived!* What great adventure would the day bring? And now . . . something had happened to the whole world. Mornings weren't filled with anticipation, just duty. Nothing took me away on a wave. The moments couldn't be collected; they just tumbled on one another, and kept coming. And birds'

singing didn't matter; nothing was intensely beautiful anymore. You had to worry about earthquakes, child abuse,
animals becoming extinct, eroding coastlines, global starva-
tion, terrorism, bigotry, the right wing, and nuclear war.
And those worries put a film over your spirit, a tint of gray
over your dreams that made them less hearty, less important, and less real.

"Brogan, let me ask you . . ." He went behind his desk
again and sat back in his chair.

Anything. I'm yours.

"Have you ever thought of . . ."

Ask, please ask!

". . . doing community work? You might enjoy it."

"Oh yes! I'm sure I would."

"Why don't I give you a couple of brochures and phone
numbers after class tomorrow?" He dug into a drawer.

"Thank you."

"You are rare, you know that?" He gave me a prime-time
smile.

Rare good, or rare weird?

I had to get out of that room before I lifted up like a
helium balloon and took my lightened consciousness, my
pitter-patter soul, and wafted out the window. I needed to
keep this talk inside me, not leak it out but let it smolder,
magnifying my life.

Rare . . . it was this day, this conversation, this connec-
tion that was rare!

He asked me to work with him. Glory!

Chapter Four

I stood opposite Rosanna at the volleyball net. I played the front, hoping to spike some mean balls. That was a simple thrill, *bam*, you could almost kill the ball and right away you'd feel a sting of pleasure. *Bam! Pass it to me, I'm ready!* My knees were bent, and I was sweating because also facing me was Pat Stone, who truly was a maniac and not only could savagely hit the ball but wouldn't care if she whipped off your head in the process. She had this lumpy, short body, and her nose needed to be arrested so the rest of her could catch up with it. She didn't shave her legs either. The girl really enjoyed looking mean.

I had on regulation shorts and socks and my hair was pinned back so I could see. Rosanna didn't look like the rest of us. There she stood, all curves, her hair running down her back.

"Come on," I said to my team, "let's win by twenty points."

"Wow, this game is so important to you," said Rosanna as I took my position and waited for the whistle.

"I just like to win. That's what sports are about."

"I don't like competition," she said, pulling up her socks.

"Then you shouldn't play."

"I'd rather swim. It's very sensual and pleasant. I prefer activities that require cooperation and harmony."

Harmony. Boy, this girl had a halo for every occasion. Was this why Mr. Price liked her—because she had no rough edges? I had hoped Mr. Price would like someone with a little more juice in her. Luckily she wasn't playing opposite Pat Stone, who could amputate her if she wanted to. Rosanna laughed when Pat set up the ball for her. She tapped it sweetly, and it sort of meandered over the net right into my capable hands. I whacked it real hard, and it landed right next to her, scoring the first glorious point for my team.

But Rosanna smiled at me like I had given her a compliment! On my team they would have booed someone missing that defense, but nobody on her team said a word. I guess people expected Rosanna to just stand there. Then she was the third in a really good setup that started in the third row, and she fumbled.

"Either slam it or pass it," commanded Pat.

Rosanna smiled.

"Don't *smile* at me," Pat growled.

For the moment, I loved Pat Stone.

Personally, I wanted to send one ace zipping past Pat Stone's head so she would know she wasn't the only terror on the court. I would pack all my energy into the ball, and *fwarp,* it would go and land on their side, and *zing,* I would feel fine and triumphant.

The ball flew around from our side to theirs; several close calls, and I sent lots to Darlene, who had a good eye. I played net like a champ. Now the ball was in the back row, and someone goofed and it went flying to Rosanna, who gave it her basic polite flick. Off it went, cockeyed.

"Get out your frustrations on the ball," Pat advised Rosanna.

"I don't have any," answered Rosanna.

"She's too beautiful to have emotions," cracked Pat. "We all know what *that's* like!"

Rosanna's face changed. "Emotions! You want emotions? Well, I've got a few," Rosanna huffed, and then she smacked that ball. It roared through the air with terrible force and the spike worked; the ball fell on our side, dead.

"Ever hear of teamwork?" muttered Pat. "I was right here with nothing to do."

"What do you want from me?" said Rosanna.

"To stop acting like a shampoo commercial!" yelled Pat.

"Leave me alone!"

Pat glared. "How'd I get with the Barbie Dolls?"

Now I served. It went right to Rosanna. Her two fists went up, and with a grunt she impacted that ball hard and even managed to set it up for the front row.

34

"Great!" shouted Pat.

"Calm down," said Rosanna. "I didn't do it for you."

Then Rosanna was server. She didn't have a strong arm, but she packed the swing as best she could and the ball went flying. It came right to me, so I pummeled it over and it volleyed a few times on both sides. Then that same serve was heading for Rosanna, and she tore up to meet it and fiercely returned the ball to make the point.

It was strange. Rosanna started playing hard. She scuffled, she flew, she pounced, she sweated, she cursed, she set the ball up, and she went half mad when she blew a point.

"Well, so the femme fatale can actually sweat," said Pat.

"I can sweat, I can be mean, I can win this game," Rosanna barked. Her hair was wet and her shirt was sweaty.

But I wanted to win too. My team made nine points while I kept the serve. Darlene passed me the ball beautifully, and in the end we were victorious by two points.

When we left the court, Pat slapped Rosanna on the back like she was one of the Boston Celtics. "You surprised me, pal," she said.

Rosanna surprised me too. Something of drastic importance was missing from my equation, wasn't it? Or was the truth simply that no matter what she said, Rosanna had plenty of rough edges, plenty of gall, plenty of rage. The only question now was, Did she hide that from Mr. Price under her coy and fetching ways, or did he know about it? I didn't like that I had to perceive her differently now.

What lay under the surface made Rosanna more of a person to me.

Price dropped another bombshell that day. That seemed to be his style. I guess that's why he operated the way he did—he had to work hard to get our attention.

There he was wearing a flecked shirt open at the neck and a loose jacket, totally stylish, and there I was wondering how he had such good taste and what it would be like to go shopping with him, when I heard him say, "Good work! You seem to understand some of Reich's thinking, and most of you seem to agree with his diagnosis that we all are personally domina ed by the values, the structures, and the consciousness of our society. Now I want you to come up with solutions as you see them. When Reich wrote this book, 'awareness' was still a new word. So was 'consciousness,' in the sense that he used it. He was responding to the degeneration that he saw, and that's what I want you to do."

Susan Seymour's hand flew up and jerked around threateningly. "I don't agree that there *is* degeneration."

"Read the newspapers," said Bruce Tailor.

"Hey, man," said Ira, "you're asking us to prescribe medicine for a very sick country. And we're not doctors."

"Exactly," said Price. "I'm asking because I want to see if we can come up with some original solutions. We all live here. Reich looked around his environment, analyzed it, thought about it, and came to conclusions. We all do that all the time, but now instead of analyzing your friends or your parents, I want you to analyze the soup you live in."

"How long do we spend on this?" asked Susan.

"All semester. You'll each pick one area and do a report."

Michelle moaned. "Can we work on this with someone else?" she asked. That meant Art, but Art would just tag along with Michelle's ideas.

"Work on your own. You have more ideas than you think, but you're distracted. That's why I'm making your whole grade depend on this project. To cut down the distraction level."

A buzz went around the class. "Unfair" was the word that predominated. The second word was "crazy." Even I thought he was going too far.

"But we're not politicians," said Susan.

"Correct. You're citizens. Like the founding fathers of this country. Look, the way to approach this is to take the most irksome problem that you see around you, the biggest flaw or contradiction, and address yourselves to that. Maybe it's lack of community. Well, start making notes about what brings people together. Use your own life. If it's competition, think about the pluses and minuses. If it's meaningless work and you don't know what meaningless work is, go get a job and see what you come up with. I don't want abstract theories. I want insights based on your lives."

"I haven't had to think in seventeen years," cracked Ira.

"Then the educational system owes you. Now, I'm going to have conferences with each of you."

Drat. I had theories, but I didn't have life. I opened the

book and started underlining. The trouble was I was underlining almost everything. Meanwhile, everyone fidgeted in their seats. Price was turning into the world's sexiest dictator.

Then he leaned over me. "This is way too hard," I whispered.

"Way too hard, just like life. Now, I found this brochure for the Meadows Recreation Center for Senior Citizens. It will help you with this assignment. If you're interested you can call Mr. Ames."

"Me?" I said stupidly.

"Let me know how it goes." He was on to Darlene.

I fondled the paper. Did he give this to anyone else? Would I call? I had to—it was my ace in the hole. "Rowland," I would say. "Let's have a cup of coffee. I'll tell you everything."

Bruce Tailor walked me down the hallway after school. "You're about the most interesting person in class," he said, not looking at me.

"But I didn't say anything today."

"I could hear you thinking." He smiled. "Loudly."

Perhaps I should get to know him better. But before I could find anything to say, he headed off to the gym.

I went directly to the bus stop. The address and phone number of the senior citizens' center was in my bag. Only Mr. Price could get me to do this. It had to bring us closer. It would show him how dedicated and down-to-earth I was.

And this experience would help illuminate the America Mr. Price was teaching us about. The one I read about in the newspapers and heard about on T.V. The country that was so demoralized its people took drugs and alcohol and beat up on little kids. Seniors had lived through so much history. I had my notebook with me. I would write down all my impressions.

I felt special on the crowded bus. Even though the driver lurched around every other turn and my stomach seemed to rise into my chest. I was going to work with Mr. Price! It was too incredible!

The two-story stucco building had balloons strung over the entrance. It reminded me of grade-school decorations. Two or three senior citizens sat outside talking. Nearby a man dozed. What would I have to say to these people? It would be like having hundreds of grandparents. They'd all tell you not to put blond in your hair and *tsk tsk* if you said anything outrageous. Or they'd all be taking yoga classes, trying tofu for the first time, and showing you their pictures of their last trip to Europe. That's what my grandparents used to be like. Then Nan's parents moved to Florida and sent baskets of oranges four times a year and pictures of themselves playing bridge. We were always supposed to visit them and never did.

Buster's mom had died and his father played the horses somewhere in Chicago. I remembered him for his big nose and cigar smoke. I hadn't seen him in years.

Now here I was, walking through the front door of Meadows Recreation Center. Facing me was a bulletin board. On it were phone numbers for roommates, and several doctors' cards; also a bingo schedule and a tour bus brochure. Decorating the hallways were various oil paint-ings apparently done in the arts class, mostly still lifes and flower arrangements. If I hadn't been going to meet my dream man I would have turned and walked out. It was depressing, and more depressing for its pathetic attempt at cheer.

I looked around for the office. Then I saw a black man walk up to me on long spindly legs. He was very thin and his features broke out on his face like flares—big eyes, big nose and mouth, big ears, and not enough face for all of them. His arm reached out to shake mine and he had a hard grasp, like it really meant something to shake your hand. I liked him immediately.

"You must be Brogan, and this here handshake belongs to me, Ames. I know, I know, this must look pretty down and out to you, but it ain't really." He laughed. "Now, before you tell me you think you made a mistake, and you really meant to be at the mall, let me drop you off at our special afternoon dance."

"When is Mr. Price coming?" I gushed.

"I don't reckon until he hits about seventy-five," laughed Ames.

What? I had completely misunderstood! This couldn't be happening to me. But Ames led me into a big room where even more balloons and crepe paper were strung across the ceiling.

I was trapped. I looked for doors and excuses.

Old people danced to an accordion player and a drum-mer who pumped out a polka.

"We mostly have Italians and Germans," explained Ames.

I didn't care if he had Martians—I had to get out of there.

"So now we've got cross-pollination: Italians who love to polka!"

An old man was heading toward us. He looked like he was going to ask me to dance! How could Mr. Price do this to me? Was this some hideous test of my moral fiber? Well then, I would fail.

"Try to keep up. Mr. Langerfeld is a real wild man," warned Ames, and he turned to leave.

"Good afternoon, miss. Caring to dance?" The old man sputtered his words, but the gaze in his eye was steady. "Be very honored." He smiled brightly, revealing a missing tooth. And I remembered my grandpa Murray, who had a crooked nose and a crooked finger, but with bright light that came from his eyes when he came to visit.

"Well, uh, I don't know how to polka," I stalled. If Michelle could see me now she'd never even speak to me again.

"Langerfeld know. Langerfeld teach you!" said the man, and he took my arm and put his hand around my waist. He smelled of tobacco, and he was wearing a pale-pink shirt that set off his deep-blue eyes. I liked that shirt, and the little bit of gel he had put on his hair so that it lay back neatly on his skull. His hands were small and brittle, but he moved with determination that bordered on glee, if someone that old could feel glee. He spun me out to the middle of the floor, getting zippier and zippier in his movements.

"You pretty girl. You dancing good, not to worry," said the man. "Nice place," he said, nodding in appreciation for this ordinary building.

"Very nice," I lied. Why didn't these people have somewhere prettier to go to?

"Yes, beautiful. I come here since I retire," said Mr. Langerfeld. "I now seventy-seven years old. Retire five years. Electrical wiring. Having good time. Wife died, now am bachelor. Girlfriend won't marry me because she say she no cook for any man ever again. She through. No iron, either. Very independent. But I like her anyway."

Mr. Langerfeld pranced me across the room.

"That's nice."

"Thursdays, dance. Wednesdays, yoga. Saturday, Ping-Pong. Sunday, cards and turkey dinner." He swirled me around, then dipped me. *"Quest' è paradiso."*

Paradiso. The polka band speeded up. So did the old man.

"Know what means *'paradiso'*?"

I shook my head no.

"My Italian friend Mr. Albiandi, see over there"—and he waved across the room to a short dark man with a mustache—"teach me new language. Means 'paradise.' *'Quest' è paradiso'* is meaning 'This is paradise.'" He waved again and shouted, "Hey, Vittore!"

Then Mr. Langerfeld took a daring little hop. He really meant what he was saying. He was in paradise, and I was in hell. Split in two. One of me felt awful. It wanted to go home. It didn't want to dance with some old man who had bad gums and broken English. The other me was curious. Were these people wise? Did they have stories to tell?

"You very pretty girl." The music built to an end.

"Thanks for the dance," I said, then I tore out of Mr. Langerfeld's spotty old arms and right out of paradise.

Chapter Five

"Là ci darem la mano . . . " an off-key but passionate bass boomed out into our front yard. Opera, as performed by my totally blasted father, no doubt. Right away I wanted to see my mother. When Buster drank, sometimes she would get a frightening calm about her, but there were other times when she would get hysterical. Other times she grew urgently philosophical like I imagined she was when she worked for civil rights in college.

I heard the pottery wheel spinning in the basement, which meant she was in the calm state for now. I rushed downstairs and sat down on a wooden box.

"Brogan, promise me you won't get married." She was completely muddy, a cigarette dangling from her lips.

"Ma . . ."

"I mean it. Promise me you won't get married and that you'll take yourself seriously."

"You mean you can't take yourself seriously if you're married?"

"It's harder."

"Hey, what's going on down there?" shouted Buster. "Come here and talk to your old man, Brogan."

I didn't want to go.

"Go," said my mother.

"Why, so he won't bother you?"

"That's an awful thing to say. He's your father and he's lonely."

Didn't she realize when Buster got too close to the bottle, she wanted me to act like her agent? I hated it, but I also secretly hoped I could do the magic trick and get him to quit, so I did what she said. "What else were you saying, Ma?" I got up to go.

"Sometimes I think he may have a serious drinking problem."

I had wondered the same thing. But what did it mean, and what did we do if it were true? "He's getting worse, isn't he?"

"Do you think so? I think he's probably just under a lot of pressure. I'd hate to think that your father's turning into an alcoholic."

I wondered if you turned into an alcoholic and if you did, what made you turn? Was it me? Or Nan? I changed the subject. "Making anything special?"

"Don't you want to talk to me, tell me about school, or

boyfriends?" boomed my dad from upstairs. "You never talk to me."

"He's lonely," repeated my mother. "Maybe if you talk to him . . ."

"In a minute," I told her. *"In a minute,"* I shouted upstairs.

I looked around Nan's studio. Unglazed vases stood in abandonment next to plates, cups, and lamp bottoms. Once I had had great hopes for my mother's career as a potter.

The only good part about my father's drinking was that my mother used me to escape and that meant she actually discussed things with me. I became her ally instead of her child.

"I don't know, I'm tired of pots. Maybe I should do something else. Something for people." She worked the clay to get rid of air bubbles. "Women need to make a real imprint on society. We need to balance it, shift the values. That's my feminist training speaking, and it's right!"

I got excited when my mother talked seriously. She'd get angry at injustice and I loved that about her. But also she wouldn't scream that my room looked like it belonged in *The Clan of the Cave Bear.*

"You should, you really should. Like what?"

"Brogan, this is not career counseling, this is just a conversation." Which meant as soon as my dad got sober she'd forget all about it.

"Damn it, Brogan! I'm home early." He paced back and forth, making the floor creak.

"Honey, you'd better go."

"Sure, send up the sacrifice."

"You do better with him when he's this way, and you know it."

Not fair. But I headed upstairs anyway.

I heard the wheel running. She could tune out. I faced my father.

"What do you two talk about down there?" He had the chips out, which meant he was planning several more drinks.

"I don't know. Nothing special."

"Well, I wish you'd talk to me," said Buster. He was almost teary.

"What's the matter, Dad?"

"What's the matter? I can't tell you what's the matter. Anyway, the market is way down. Whatever I buy drops. My damn broker tells me it'll come back up."

"Maybe it will."

He poured himself another drink.

"Some things come back up, and some things just keep going down," he said philosophically. "Down, down, down."

"Dad, you sounded happy before. You were singing."

"You liked my singing?" he said almost like a little kid.

"Yes. Sure I did. It's an opera, right?"

"Opera has all the great passions, Brogan. You should listen sometime. *Don Giovanni* is one of the greats." And he started singing again, his eyes rolling, and his chest heaving. I stayed for a while and encouraged him. Don Giovanni. That was Don Juan.

Then I went back downstairs. "You realize that someday your dad and I are going to get divorced," said Nan; then her knee hit the button, and the wheel went swirling around.

I wanted to shout, "Wait!" I wanted to tell her that the word—divorce—was something I lived with along with other important words like death, or college, or love . . . or alcoholic. Big words. Big, big words. But divorce, well, that was something you could do something about, wasn't it? Something you had control over, something, if you tried hard enough, you could avoid. But the wheel was noisy, and if I stayed I would only keep getting flecked with clay.

Mr. Price walked into class the next day wearing a tan blazer, gray shirt, and baggy pants. I closed my eyes to memorize everything. Rosanna wore a flower in her hair and high-heeled shoes. When he called her name he looked up for a second. When he called my name he looked up too. I would thank him for sending me to the Recreation Center. I would tell him it expanded my horizons. I would not say anything about being tricked.

"I hope you're all ready to put down what your topic is so we can make sure there are no duplications."

"This guy Reich was just a hippie with a pencil," said Susan Seymour. "He says the 'new consciousness' people don't care about the right colleges or the right jobs. So then 'old consciousness' means 'yuppies.' "

"Maybe you should discuss that! The similarities between the 1950's and the 1980's."

"Piece of cake."

"Good," said Mr. Price. "Who else?"

"I'd like to discuss feminism as an underlying and contributing factor to the issues in *The Greening of America*," I said.

"Feminism per se isn't discussed in Reich's book," said Mr. Price patiently.

"I know. But Reich discusses the lack of power people have over their lives. The population that has had the *most* lack of power is women. If Reich had written this book today, I bet he would have included it."

"We are reading the book exactly as it was written," said Price. "Talk to me after class."

Just what I'd hoped for, a private tête-à-tête. I slipped on a little lipstick and fluffed my hair. In other words, I acted like a dumb girl so that I could come off as a smart one who was extremely cute.

But after the bell rang, when I began to talk, I forgot how I looked. Impassioned, I explained to him that if you were a woman living now, there was one main thing that shaped your life and that was male domination. As he shuffled his papers he laughed, and said he wouldn't give in.

I stood there thinking that he was dead wrong, and that I didn't care what he said. Because I had seen my mother threatening divorce and my father drunk too many times.

Chapter Six

Monday afternoon I was on my way to the Meadows Rec
Center again. I had to make my impression on Mr. Price
indelible ... had to show him how incredibly different I was
from everyone else, and that inside me beat the heart of a
concerned citizen.

Sure I had vowed never to return. But now I had no
choice. How could I convince Mr. Price to let me deviate
from the curriculum unless he viewed me as a "Consciousness Three" person, someone self-determined, free, and
concerned with humanity. MRC was the ticket.

I walked into the center, which smelled of macaroni
mixed with the glue of the arts and crafts room. A new set
of poignant primitive oil paintings hung in the hallways.

Ames peeked out of his office and waved me in. "So you

came back," he bellowed. His smile told me he had expected no less.

"The ladies put on a fashion show every year," he explained. "Many of them sew nicely, but a few of them have a little trouble with their eyesight. Sometimes they forget where they put things. Sometimes they need a little help with the pinning, or picking out some fabric. Or you could cut the patterns out for them if you like.

"Sometimes, they just get a kick out of seeing a younger person in the environment. Understand?" He smiled that grin of his that absolutely engraved itself between your eyes and seemed to mean you were friends for life. "Just bring them your twinkle," he said with his twinkle, and led me upstairs.

Twinkle! I walked up the stairs like Joan of Arc, about to make a great sacrifice. Ames didn't notice; he whistled as he strode into a room filled with several sewing machines, mirrors, and bulletin boards tacked with patterns.

"Here she is!" he boomed to everyone. There was something ancient about a bunch of women fussing over clothes as they were. Some were going through pattern books, some were examining material, some were measuring their hips and groaning.

One woman nearly knocked me over. She had pins in her mouth and was wearing a pattern over her dress. "Shorry," she said, her lips squeezed together.

Michelle would be appalled if she knew where I was. On the other hand, she belonged here more than I did. Only yesterday, she was pestering me about matching or contrasting accessories. "Accessories" was such an unfeminist word, I couldn't even say it.

"Michelle, in the larger scheme of things, it's low. Like earthworms are more important," I had told her.

"Maybe to earthworms, earthworms are important, but to me accessories are important and they should be to you too instead of going crazy over feminism, which isn't even in the book."

"If it were in the book, it wouldn't be a problem."

"Right. Now I won't feel taken advantage of if we can get back to my feelings about mauve. Belt, stockings, scarf, you think?"

Now one of the women held out a box of straight pins. "Darling, maybe you wouldn't mind giving me darts."

I pinned the back panel, and handed it back to her.

"What kind of dress will you make?" I asked a lady who was knitting with tremendous intensity.

"Oy, don't ask her," said one of the other ladies.

But the woman answered. "No dress for me. I am knitting a world event, an afghan that will eventually reach across the United States. Women will knit it together."

This woman didn't look like the others; she had very closely cropped gray hair and wore one big earring. Even though she was probably in her late sixties, if you squinted, her face also looked about fourteen. Sometimes I think everyone is frozen at one single age. If you study a person you can make it out. Our bodies obey the laws of physics but our minds obey the laws of emotions, and emotions seem to freeze. My Aunt Mina lost a finger when she was seven, and you can see seven-year-old Mina if you look. That's my game, guessing the real age of folks. Only a few people are ever their real age, and fewer still are those who are ninety who are *really* ninety, though I suspect the older you succeed in getting, the less you are a baby. Like Carl Jung or Georgia O'Keeffe were probably really ninety years old in the true sense. I told this theory to my mother and she howled. "Write it down," she advised, "so one day you can laugh too."

Anyway, this woman was slight and dainty, and she didn't really fit into this group. She wore a peace pin on her blouse, and bright marine-blue eye shadow that made her big, brown eyes look beautiful.

"Don't listen to her," said the woman with pins in her mouth. "Oh, hello, I'm Ruth."

"I'm Brogan."

Ruth pumped my hand as if she were running for political office. She had lots of style.

"May," a short, plump woman shook my hand. Her hair was sprayed so much it could have been a helmet. She also had a big, engaging grin with a gap between her teeth that made her look very friendly.

"My name is Maria." A lady with a big blond streak in her dark hair smiled at me. "And that's . . . that's Gracie."

"Women have been oppressed for seven million years," said Gracie without missing a stitch.

"Last week you said it was eight million," said May. "Which is it?"

"Seven million years."

"I wasn't oppressed by *my* husband," said Ruth. "He was a wonderful man. A little boring sometimes—who could care about a stationery store the way he did? Men get so involved in their businesses—but not oppressed."

"Antonio got *too* involved," said Maria.

Everyone waited for an explanation, but she didn't say anymore.

"All women have been oppressed," repeated Gracie.

Ruth turned to me. "We call her Crazy Gracie. You remember George Burns's wife? He loved her for so long."

"Not for seven million years," said Gracie.

"Say good night, Gracie," said Maria.

Gracie's chair suddenly swiveled around. "Who thought up the Second World War? The same system that dominates woman pits man against nature, and against *himself.* We cannot live like this any longer. And what do you think, young lady?"

Was she kidding? Was it possible? She sounded like me! Here, of all places! I closed my eyes for a minute to thank myself for coming back. "Of course I think you're right!"

"Of course? I haven't heard 'of course' too much lately when I talk, but yes, I'm right! And girls your age must be aware. Did you know in another life you were served up in a slave market like lemonade?" Gracie's eyes bored into my face. "Now a boy says jump, and you leap."

"I'm *not* like that," I said defiantly. "I'm completely against that!"

Gracie shook her head disbelievingly.

"Don't get upset over Gracie," whispered Maria.

54

"Look, dear, I want to make a nice skirt," said May. "You got anything with dots?"

I went over to the rolls of fabric and started looking.

"Dots, May?" said Ruth as if May had just announced she were going topless.

"You don't read *Vogue,*" said Ruth without looking up. "*Vogue* is nothing but dots."

"*Vogue* is for thin young women with bulging pocketbooks, not for fat old women with skinny ones."

"Got any dots?" May smoothed out her pattern with calm determination.

The pile of cloth was a potpourri of things probably donated from a fabric shop. I pulled out a print with dots and triangles and handed it to May, who began to spread it over the pattern.

"Dots or no dots, as a woman you're still no threat to the status quo," said Gracie. "You're just an object."

"Shhh, Gracie," said Ruth. "This young woman didn't come here to hear your theories." Ruth turned to me. "She read a few books once and that was it for her. Now me, I want something without pleats. Pleats make you hippy and I'm already hippy." She pointed to a drawing in the pattern book. For a minute, it was as if Michelle had been stuck in a time machine and reappeared as an old lady.

"Ruth, that isn't pleats, it's only shirring," said May.

I began cutting.

"It wasn't only one book, it was dozens. Starting with Simone de Beauvoir up to the recent ones," corrected Gracie.

"That's why today we sit here with a genius," said Ruth.

"I'll be on the Carson show," said Gracie. "He likes old people. I'll let him knit a piece of the afghan, but he'll be the only man who's allowed."

"I'm sure he'll drop everything to learn how to knit," said Maria.

"I'm glad you understand *something,*" said Gracie, missing the sarcasm. "This Maria, in case you don't know, has a *voice.* Sing for this girl," she commanded Maria.

Maria shook her head. "I stopped singing a long time ago."

"Tony made her stop. Then he went to Sicily, after she cooked all the meals, raised the children, cleaned the house, and forgot her own voice . . . and he never came back! This is how it goes with us. We don't know what we want? How could we? Does a five-year-old know? Seven million years of not knowing, and I was the same way," said Gracie, knitting furiously.

"Oh, she was a beautiful singer." May turned to me. "She sang at Christmas last year. Why don't you sing something?" she asked Maria gently.

"Why not, a little tune," pleaded Ruth.

"Now he's gone and you should sing," said Gracie.

"He loved her a long time," Ruth defended her friend, whose eyes were shiny and blinking.

"Not long enough for her to give up her soul," said Gracie, unperturbed. " 'Cause nobody can ever love you that long, not even my Sol, who loved me to the day he died.

I followed the directions on the package of society, but still it wasn't enough." Gracie shook her head. "So Maria, sing already!"

Maria pushed back her hair self-consciously, then looked at all of them one by one to see if they were letting her off the hook. They weren't.

"Okay, okay, a little concert." Maria stood up and smoothed out her dress, and hummed a few notes quietly to herself. I wondered what I was in for. A screechy soprano and strained high C's and millions of verses and no escape?

She took a breath. *"Maria . . . "*

Her voice pierced the room like an exquisite laser. Silky and polished tones flowed effortlessly. She was a consummate singer and showed absolutely no strain, rather the contrary—a quite extraordinary gift. People from the hallway gravitated to the open door.

"Maria."

In front of me Maria was transformed. Her dark eyes flashed with drama, her personal power was suddenly unassailable as a banquet of sound filled the room.

I had to wonder why she hadn't used this gift. Was it as Gracie had said, that Tony didn't want her to sing? Was this yet another casualty of male dominance?

We listened in a fever until in a final flourish of quiet but explosive feeling she reached the end. Gracie might be a very opinionated old lady, I was thinking, but her opinions were good. Why had God given Maria that voice if He didn't want her to use it?

Applause erupted and stayed at a pitch, then quieted down to an almost reverent silence.

The next day before class, I hunkered over my paper, wondering what to say when Mr. Price announced we were to report on our progress.

"How about you, Susan?" he asked. You always had to call on Susan first, or else she would catapult out of her seat.

She was ready to answer. "Reich is the most judgmental, pretentious . . . saying people ski because they think they *should* ski. How does *he* know?"

"He's describing Consciousness Two," said Bruce.

"Consciousness Two," said Art, "says society fails to address certain interests. I'd say that's true. My dad came back from 'Nam using drugs and alcohol."

"Art!" Michelle whispered. She chewed on a pencil and I could see she was embarrassed.

"Well, I know all you amateur sociologists are going to be amazed when you hear that I took a part-time job waiting tables," said Ira. "It's not bad when you consider I hear great jokes and eat fresh lasagna."

Good. Maybe Ira would get fat and ugly.

"Restaurants tell us lots about a culture," said Mr. Price.

Rosanna's hand floated up. "Reich says change must come through culture. So I am learning an old classical Spanish dance about the struggle of the *paisan'*."

I raised my hand before I could fume over the picture of Mr. Price drooling over Rosanna in frilly skirts. "You can't discuss these issues without discussing women, since what we are talking about is the result of a male-dominated system."

Ira held his pencil like a microphone. "And so, welcome to the Gloria Steinem talk show. . . ."

Mr. Price was silent.

Everyone looked at me. Suddenly I felt choked up and squinty eyed. I saw it all so clearly . . . I felt The Problem everywhere—in me, outside me, in the ads I saw, the clothing I wore, in my mother and father's life, in the way Mr. Price looked at Rosanna. Didn't Price realize we were all sinking together?

"Please . . . " I said. "I really want to write about feminism. If our culture treated women with dignity and respect, there would be more of a balance. After all, corporate America, which Reich implicates as one of the main problems, is male."

Price shook his head no.

"Imelda Marcos sings the blues," said Ira on his fake mike.

"If she had been able to develop herself, she probably wouldn't have become so greedy," I said. Ira pretended to fall off his chair.

I looked right into Mr. Price's eyes. "You're just part of the male establishment, no different from a corporate executive, wielding male power," I said. "Except instead of material exploitation, in this case it's something worse: mind control."

"Go, Brogan, go, the hole is getting deeper," said Ira.

"Brogan, you are way out of line." Mr. Price was calm.

"Do you really think that's what men are about?" asked Bruce Tailor.

"I think men practiced subjugating women and now men are subjugating each other," I said. "Except women are the ones who are underpaid."

"Well, I think she *should* be allowed to write about this issue," said a petulant Michelle. My friend Michelle!!!

"You don't have to be an underpaid *anything* unless that's what you choose. You have to fight for what's right." Mr. Price's face had turned stony and wasn't even remotely handsome.

"That's what I'm *trying* to do!" I spluttered.

And I thought of Maria and her choices. What is a real choice, anyway? You have to be free to choose both in your mind and in reality, otherwise all you do is slip or slide into an alternative.

"Why can't she pursue this?" asked Bruce.

If Mr. Price shot me down now, I'd stay down and I'd become mean and rebellious. I stared at an ink spot on my desk and pleaded with it to get the right answer.

"You are challenging the system," said Mr. Price, shifting from foot to foot. "In this case the system happens to be me. Now Mr. Reich thinks it's very important for the future of this country that we learn to think in an original way. So in that spirit, which is the foundation of *The Greening of America*, I feel justified in granting you your topic. See me after class and I'll suggest some reading."

All right!

I loved Mr. Price more than ever. Except, drat, I had

60

embarrassed him in front of the class. He must hate me. But he *can't* hate me. He must admire me for my spirit. Rowland, I'll read every book on feminism I can find, and you'll be so proud!

The thing is, I *shouldn't* care at all what he thinks. I should care what *I* think. Isn't that the whole point of feminism, to redefine ourselves from the inside, to rebalance our culture? Then why do I care so much about *him*? It's wrong, *all wrong*! Unless it's that I want to be *really* me and be liked at the very same time. Or is it that I'm just a pushover and I need approval the way a mop needs dirt?

Chapter Seven

"We're buying a dress today," Michelle announced as she escorted me to her favorite store in the mall. "Even feminists like to look good *sometimes*. I saw a picture of Bella Abzug's house: lots of closets and plenty of mirrors."

"Don't you love these rhinestones? God, I love them." Michelle had opinions about everything that came in boxes, and I had opinions about everything that didn't.

"Michelle, I'm only coming to this party because it's yours."

"And when you're necking with some gorgeous guy, you can tell them you're doing *that* for me too!"

If I ever got to neck with Mr. Price, it wouldn't be for Michelle. "Necking?!" I squeaked. "I don't even like anyone."

"That's the problem . . . whoops!" She stopped walking. "Look who's there."

It was Rosanna and her sister carrying shopping bags from various stores.

"She's gorgeous," I said.

Michelle shrugged. "If you like that type."

"You mean the gorgeous flawless type?"

That was the type Mr. Price liked. Why couldn't we choose who we wanted to look like? Why'd we have to be born in this indelible way? What was the use if your soul was good but your nose was ugly, or your hair, or your ears? It was like God was playing a joke. Everyone I knew had a glitch. My aunt Rachael could sing, but she had thin hair and no breasts. My mother cared about politics and was beautiful, but wasn't happy. Everyone on the planet seemed to be a walking "what's-wrong-with-this-picture?" Except for someone like Rosanna. What could a new dress do for me that God hadn't already built in for Rosanna?

"Come on." Michelle hauled me into The Limited and threw a yellow dress in my face. "Pretend you're drop-dead stunning. Make my day." She shoved me into a dressing room.

It was pretty, I had to admit, but my face went green against the color. I pulled off the lemon jersey number, getting into the spirit. "Be right back," I told her, and zoomed out and found a scarlet sheath with a cut-out back. I modeled it by swishing around and swinging my hair. Was Gloria Steinem like this, opinionated and impassioned until you got her into a department store? Did she suddenly defect into Victoria Principal the minute you put something trendy in her hands?

"Scarlet is your color! And little black heels with rhinestones—*yes,* you're taking it!" Michelle didn't even try to control her enthusiasm.

It looked nice on me, I had to admit.

"Contrary to popular opinion, my best friend is not a mental case," Michelle said as she dumped the dress on the sales counter. The saleslady twittered and rang it up.

I loved the way the color set off my hair and eyes. We walked out of the store together, me with a little kick of excitement that would have lasted the rest of the day—if on the escalator I hadn't spotted Mr. Price, going up as we were going down. I ducked.

"That's who you have the crush on, isn't it?" Michelle smiled slyly.

"You must be kidding," I said, standing up again, and gave her my most incredulous look.

"Very interesting," said Michelle. "One sure way to get an A."

"I just think he's got a good mind."

"Sure," said Michelle. "Tell it to his wife."

"Is he married?"

"He was last year when my sister had him. But maybe it's like in the book—he believes in living outside the system."

Married? No, it couldn't be. Not my Mr. Price. He just couldn't be married—it would ruin everything. "He'd better be careful," I said ominously, as if I could do anything about it. "He'd better be careful."

When I got home my mother was at her desk studying something. "I'm deciding who to work for," she said, looking up. "I could go back to NOW and support the ERA, volunteer to support my congressman on child care . . ." Her voice faltered.

"You're crying."

She was sniffing away.

"Is it Dad?"

"No, today it's just me. Feeling sorry for myself. Searching for my core."

"Searching for your core is good."

"I know, but I can't find it. I had it once."

"I know you did. But Mom, society doesn't want women to have a core, see, because then we won't serve the establishment."

"Jesus, Brogan! Talking to you is like talking to Mao Tse-tung, dammit. Sometimes it's too hard to care about the big picture. Maybe that's why I'm having such trouble deciding. Isn't my own soul important?"

But we don't live according to our souls, I wanted to say, we live according to T.V. advertisements. "I'm sorry, Mom." I went over to her and hugged her but she shooed me away.

Life can't be this hard and people can't be this defeated. Nan's gloom frightened me. I didn't want to inherit it.

"I'll make a decision and then I'll feel better," she said

after a while. She went downstairs to her potting wheel.

But then she'd want to run away again.

Something in me tells me you can't run away. It doesn't work. You have to run *toward* your soul. If I see my soul anywhere, no matter where, I must run toward it, and run fast or I will lose it in a carnival of priorities, as women always have.

I showed off the dress at dinner.

"Sexy," said Buster.

"Sophisticated," said my mother.

"Very sexy. Turn around," said Buster. "You have a nice little behind on you."

The more he said, the stranger I felt. Why couldn't he just say in a plain and simple way that I looked pretty?

"Guess what!" Michelle's voice was breathy, curvy, filled with the adrenaline of Radio Free Gossip. "There was a sighting in the mall. Right after we left, Ira was buying those leather Nikes, and since he's a narrow . . . well anyway, he bumped into Rosanna and her sister."

"That doesn't exactly sound like satellite headlines."

"I didn't *get* to the headlines yet. I was working to set up atmosphere and tension. Okay, so Mr. Price was with them, and they were buying sneakers together."

"Juicy stuff, Michelle, but I've got to go. I have conditioner on my hair and I'm about to turn into an oil slick. 'Bye."

I hung up. My hair wasn't wet, but my body was an

electrical storm. I lay down on the bed. Hadn't I suspected this deep down? So I couldn't be crushed—I was too smart, too ahead of the game, too cynical, too much a feminist.

Things will always come to Rosanna like this. Where I have to stand in line, she will be whisked through the private entrance. She is one of those girls for whom the rules do not apply. She will break hearts while hers stays intact.

I wanted to shake Mr. Price. I wanted to wipe out Rosanna. I wanted to invent some other God.

Chapter Eight

I was sick with imaginings: Rosanna having dinner with Mr. Price, his devotion washing over her like sea waves, she making him crazy with the angles of her beauty. He sees nothing, no one, but her. Is she flattered? Can she see him the way I do? If she is earnest, how long will that last? After all, he's got to be at least thirteen years older than she is. Will she get tired of him? It might take him centuries to get tired of measuring perfection.

If I could only talk to Michelle. If I lied and said Mr. Price was someone else, someone from the summer, she could come up with fantastic solutions: Make him jealous, send him your picture in a sexy dress, whisper to him on the phone. Silly, puerile ideas.

Michelle didn't understand this longing because she always filled her last boyfriend's spot instantly, as if she were hiring someone for a plum job. For her, boys were replaceable, a prescription that was easy to fill.

At one point I casually said, "What do you think of Price? Cute, isn't he?"

"I knew it! You *do* like him. But you can't fool around with a teacher."

"I only asked if you thought he was cute."

"He's not my type. And he's not yours either. Our types are seventeen to twenty years old, and they like dancing and pizza and fast cars. Why would you like him, anyway?"

"Just that he cares so much about everything. He's got such great morals. I bet he's writing a book."

"He drives a new two-seater car and he probably wants to be a male model. And as far as his morals go, care to explain why he was hanging around with one of his students?"

"Trying to help. Ever think of that?" I said.

"Help."

"How do you know?" I was almost yelling. "Mr. Price is community minded."

"Right up there with you and Gandhi," said Michelle. "It's a good thing Gandhi is dead. I couldn't bear to hear you had a crush on *him*!"

"I don't have crushes," I said vehemently. "Anyway, you're right. Mr. Price is too old."

I couldn't tell her I finally knew a man I could admire. And the discussion was over.

This longing—it was not feminist. The true feminist

longed only to be herself. But me, there wasn't *enough* of myself yet. I wanted to be consumed, filled, joined with someone else. With him.

Now I went into my mother's studio to throw pots. The wheel spun and spun, and I felt the clay willing to obey me. Whether is was wet, slippery, thin, or thick, I was the master of it; even if I wobbled or slipped, the clay obeyed. The wheel made the clay my slave, even if my creations were wildly lopsided. The prospects were endless, but finally the clay was not. I loved the finitude of clay, just the opposite of thought. I prayed to think only of clay, to make a perfect pot, the way my mother had shown me. I prayed to be absorbed in the music on the radio, to forget all my ideas, to stay there for one hour and make pots, then destroy them. Then make more. Just me and this element of the earth—together we were so pure. I would mold these pots the way I wanted to be molded by Mr. Price. I would put all the love of creation into my hands and the pots would come out beautiful. Eventually, I would not think of Mr. Price.

It took nearly two hours, and I was hungry when I was done, but it worked!

My father was in the kitchen when I went in for a snack.

"You're all muddy," he said, loading the fridge with beer from the pantry.

"I like mud."

He snorted, and picked out one of the cold beers that lay ready in wait for him. Then he opened it and searched for his heavy glass mug. "Tell me what's so great about mud," he challenged me, sitting down on a stool. "I'm all ears."

Once in a while Buster became fascinated by me. I always fell for it. Maybe this time he would hear me and know me; he would see me and like what he saw. I took a breath.

"Well, it's . . ." I started to say "sensuous" but I stuttered. That was not a word I could say to Buster. "It's basic," I said. "And you have a feeling you are with a primitive part of the earth. So you feel connected."

My father held up his mug and toasted me. "To connecting."

"Dad, maybe you'd like to come to the studio and throw a few pots? I could show you how."

He threw back his head and laughed almost merrily.

"It'll be fun!" I wished I had a father who could look to me for the little pieces of life I knew about.

"Why don't you fix your hair?" Suddenly his mood changed.

"My hair?"

Now he didn't answer, just sucked on his beer.

"What's wrong with my hair?"

"Grow it or cut it or curl it or color it. Hell, I don't know. It looks like a bird's nest, a crazy old bird's nest."

"You don't like the way I look?"

He didn't answer.

"Dad . . ." My voice came out a whine. I didn't like how I felt or sounded, yet moments before I'd been buoyant and exhilarated. "Tell me what you mean!"

He threw the can against the wall and it splattered sticky

beer all over me and the kitchen counter, then bounced noisily several times before it stationed itself under the stove. This seemed to give him a great deal of pleasure. An awful grin broke out on his face.

I stared at him.

He shrugged, grabbed another can, and poured it into his sacred mug, which he took out on the porch to nurse. I thought I heard him mumble something about "tension" as he thumped down into a chair.

I looked at the mirror that backed the kitchen clock. I did not look right for him. If I had a voluptuous body, catlike eyes, and long wavy hair, *then* could I tell him about mud?

Unbeautiful, I made a sandwich.

I went back to my room, which was studded with books. Titles Mr. Price had recommended included *The Cinderella Complex, Women Who Love Too Much, The Wounded Woman, Kiss Sleeping Beauty Good-bye,* and *Memoirs of a Dutiful Daughter.* They were piled near my bed waiting to be read. I needed an arsenal of knowledge to feed my vague theories and piecemeal observations. Now right here on the floor were the chartered flights of women who'd fled oppression both inner and outer. I would become their foot soldier in the revolution.

For example, Simone de Beauvoir, the great author, had been head over heels in love with her cousin Jacques, a total loser! Given to extremes in all ways, searching for the truth, she had been terribly troublesome to her family: "No one would take me just as I was," she wrote in *Memoirs of a Dutiful Daughter,* "no one loved me. I shall love myself enough, I thought, to make up for this abandonment by everyone. Formerly, I had been quite satisfied with myself, but I had taken very little trouble to increase my self-knowledge; from now on, I would stand outside myself, watch over and observe myself."

She did not want an easy existence, only an authentic one. I turned off my light at four in the morning.

The next day, Saturday, I hardly left my room. I was hooked. De Beauvoir's Sorbonne studies, her historic meeting with Sartre, her friendships, her thoughts—I took furious notes, underlined, starred, and scribbled in the margins until they looked like another book altogether. I was so delirious from the stimulation of her intellect that as soon as I was finished with one book, I plunged into the next.

My hunger to understand had found a feast. I read in *The Wounded Woman* all about fathers and daughters. Men had devalued their daughters for so long, it had caused females to role-play. The roles were terrible, like the "dutiful daughter" (the title of yet another de Beauvoir book!), the Amazon, and the doll. I found myself in all of them! Yes, I would read, I would understand, I would grow. My struggles would become clear. One day I would be free of my father's view of women, and free from Nan's defeat.

Saturday night my parents asked if I wanted to go to a movie. I said I preferred to stay home.

"I don't get you. You could be out having fun, maybe

even getting into a little trouble!" Buster winked. "Instead, you're studying to be a misfit."

I didn't need to study to be a misfit. That was something I simply was. But what I had found out these last hours was that some of the best people were misfits. I was hardly alone.

Buster and Nan went out early. I ran a steamy bath, put on my warm robe and fuzzy slippers, and ate ice cream and wisdom.

Chapter Nine

I slipped into my seat just as the bell rang. Michelle was dressed entirely in pale peach, which was quite a feat, and her hair sat on top of her head in an arrangement that begged to be exported to the Mardi Gras. Still, I had to admit she looked good. Rosanna, however, wore a pajamas-looking outfit with no waistline, and her hair hung in an MTV tangle. I wished I'd spent more time getting dressed that morning, but though I'd gotten up early, it was to read.

Price looked up from his desk and gave us a mischievous smile. "How's everyone doing with the book?" No one answered. "Price to Earth, Price to Earth . . ."

I wondered if he knew how cute he was, and if he flirted with all his classes like he was doing with us. Was this his way of teaching or did he think he was taking a screen test?

"One of Reich's theses is that people lack a deep sense of self, roots, and community. Let's examine this idea by looking at our parents. Who in this room thinks their parents lead a rich and satisfying life?"

Several kids raised their hands. Most did not.

"My parents work too hard," said Darlene, "but they own their own shop. It's very personal and it's theirs, and they like that."

"My parents do sports, they go to church, and my mother shows people around museums," said Susan.

"My parents travel," said Bruce proudly. "They love each other. They both work hard and they're very political—they haven't given up their ideals."

"To me, at this time in history, satisfaction isn't enough. We also must work to improve conditions on the planet," I said. "If you can feel good knowing kids are starving to death, or black people are being exploited, or bombs are being tested, then you're a selfish and small human being. But Reich doesn't get to talk about this. Everything in his book is based on the individual. It's a very male mentality."

"Maybe you ought to date more, Brogan," said Ira. "Some guy who bakes bread and stuff like that." He waved his arms around him, and people laughed.

"Ira, why do you think you like to wear purple shirts and pink pants? You like them because they're fun to look at. Well, guess what: Your eye for fashion comes from your feminine side. Everyone has both, you know," I told him.

"Man, am I glad I wore these today," he said. "I'm off

the hook. But basically my feminine side is with the cheer-leaders at halftime during the football season. And you're just down on guys because you don't have one."

"She could have one if she wanted one," said Michelle.

"We're off the subject here," interjected Mr. Price.

"I'm getting back to it," I said. "See, if men don't value their own tender, nurturing, spontaneous sides, then they become alienated from themselves, and the depersonaliza-tion Reich talks about in the book sets in. Everything turns out to be about power."

"What about your father?" asked Mr. Price.

"My father? My father is both a victor of capitalism and its victim. Victor because he makes money. Victim because the pressure is too much and he can't handle it."

"Wait." Susan Seymour was out of her seat again. "You're saying that if men valued their female side they would automatically take care of building public libraries or conserve the coastline?" she asked.

"For starters. And it would stop war."

The class went berserk. Ira swore he wasn't getting a sex change, then someone said he'd already had one.

Price loved every second of it. When the bell rang, he came over to my desk.

"You led us in a completely different direction. But I thought it was worthwhile," he said.

"I spent the weekend with great minds," I explained.

"Great minds who hate men?"

"No! That's not the point!"

"Good. But maybe you should hang out with some

guys. Then the theories would get a little softer." He winked.

On the way home, Michelle pestered me with questions about her party. It was this coming Friday. Should she try to serve hot food, or pizza, or just have chips and desserts? Should she decorate or not? Should she have candles all over the house to be really elegant, or just use dimmers? I answered haphazardly. My new friendship with de Beauvoir assured me she would have felt just as distant as I did.

Then, over Cokes, Michelle asked if I believed all the stuff I said in class. "Because sometimes with Art . . ."

"You mean he's a male chauvinist?"

"I didn't say that! And don't *you* say it! You know, all your radical ideas—they're not that attractive."

"Since when is thinking supposed to be a cosmetic?"

Michelle groaned. "I slept with him. I don't feel right about it. I don't know why I did it and I don't want it to happen again, but I don't know how to keep it from happening."

"Pressure," I said.

"Please, I'm begging you—don't talk like a survey."

"I'm sorry. Drat, Michelle, I don't know what to say."

"I always thought it would be so great. It wasn't that great . . . because I was so confused. I'm frightened, Brogan."

I grabbed her hand. "He's crazy about you—don't worry," I assured her. But I felt nervous for her.

"Well," she brightened, "you'll be happy to hear that Mr.

Price's birthday is the same day as mine. I invited him to my party."

"He's not coming, though, right?"

"He said he'd make an exception and stop by for a few minutes."

Mr. Price was going to be at Michelle's! I stopped worrying about her and started worrying about me. If he brought a date, I'd buy a coffin.

Putting together my outfit reminded me of Simone de Beauvoir when she was in love with her cousin Jacques. De Beauvoir loved Jacques completely. Even though he sometimes didn't act like it, she believed he was her destiny and she would never love another man. But no matter how fanatically she loved him, she also knew she had her own destiny to live out, her own questions to answer. She would not grow up to be a dependent person, someone's wife, who wasn't really real in the world. And how can you be real to yourself unless you are real in the world? Being grown up has to mean facing the world straight on, doesn't it? But if you fall all over yourself trying to make someone love you, then everything you do is for or about him. Then who you are to yourself grows dimmer. You become a satellite, and then you fade even more into the kind of woman I didn't want to be. That's why there have been so few woman artists, writers, and philosophers throughout history—women were busy being loved by men who were those things, but they didn't have the courage or the vision or the child care to be those things themselves.

Was I like de Beauvoir, really independent deep down inside no matter whom she longed for? Or was I like other women, ready to cave in to male society just to feel secure? How could I claim to be a feminist, when truly the most important thing to me was not how good my paper was for class, not what I would grow up to be, but how good I looked for Mr. Price?

Good old Michelle had brought me a makeup kit. She had showed me how to curl my hair with a curling iron, and she had forced me to go buy giant bangle earrings to go with the scarlet dress. "You have to date," she'd said to me, panic in her voice. "Otherwise you won't be *normal.* So what's wrong with Peter Druz? He's handsome. *Everyone* thinks he's handsome."

"Yuch."

"There must be somebody! What about Bruce Tailor? He likes you."

"Michelle, I don't want to *date*," I nearly screamed. "I mean, I want to be in *love*."

Thursday I was due back at the Recreation Center. I took my books on the bus for company.

The minute I got inside, Gracie spotted the beaten-up de Beauvoir paperback.

"If I could have chosen anyone to meet in my lifetime," she said, knitting her afghan, "that would have been the woman. So I am lucky, because I did."

"You actually met her! How?"

Gracie kept on knitting until I wanted to tear the needles

from her hands. She took her time; then she said, "I lived in Paris after I left Poland. I went to a lecture of hers at the Sorbonne. Afterward I introduced myself."

"Was she dressed frumpy?"

"Now that I think about it, I'd say modestly dressed. An old tweed jacket. She was serious, straightforward, sincere. She was very alive. As I stood in front of her, my own ambivalences crowded in on me, then dropped to the floor. We shook hands—it was only an instant, you understand—but I will never forget her."

I breathed in every word Gracie spoke.

"Of course, I would have liked to have met Anna Freud, too." Her needles slapped together. "Sexton the poet—now she was a good woman with a bad attitude. *Horrible.* Same with poor Virginia Woolf and Janis Joplin."

"*You* know about *Janis Joplin?*" I gasped.

"Women waste themselves," said Gracie without missing a stitch.

"I *love* Janis Joplin."

Gracie closed her eyes. "We're going to make news—good news." She closed her eyes. "I can see the headlines."

"*Mama mía,*" said Maria. "Old ladies making news. Front page, I should think?"

"Front page, large type," laughed Gracie.

Chapter Ten

I didn't see anything wrong with long brown hair, all one length with a side part, but Michelle had strong feelings about it, which was why I was sitting in the PeterPeter Salon. I was accompanied by powerful trepidations. Usually I trimmed my own hair, allowing for strange wisps to escape, but the long bangs covering my large forehead were positively nonnegotiable.

"We must communicate." Peter wore a bright-yellow shirt and trendy hair. "Communication is the most important thing," he said as if proclaiming an unheard-of truth.

"I hate short bangs," I began.

"You have a lot of energy, don't you? Well, relax," he said, and suddenly having a lot of energy seemed like a very bad thing.

"I like having a lot of energy," I said defensively.

"You ought to try T.M.," he said, and he turned me away from the mirror. "It improves the quality of your energy."

"Yes, well, are you going to cut the top or the back?"

Peter didn't fiddle around with my hair. Instead he looked at me distractedly. "Well, we can sit here all day and discuss ideas, but finally you have to take a risk." Peter was tall and muscular and seemed to think he was handsome, which he was, but in a way I didn't like.

"I'm not someone who's afraid of risks," I said uncomfortably. "Look, I have funny cheeks. I need width here." I pointed to my temples.

"I'm going to design a great look for you. You'll love it," he said.

He began rolling up my hair in tiny rollers. "I'm going to change the texture of your hair."

"*What* are you doing?"

"Look at the T.V.," he commanded. A horrible litany of MTV videos played mercilessly.

"A perm?" I said hysterically. "I don't need a perm. I *hate* curly hair!"

"Your hair needs a lift. It needs life."

I sat sullenly. I had silky hair, and maybe it wasn't as thick as Rosanna's, but when you touched it, it was smooth and luxurious.

"Trust me," he commanded.

Now I wondered if I was someone who didn't trust people. That seemed like a terrible thing. "I don't want a perm."

The videos moved furiously, and out of sync to a radio station. The effect was hypnotic. Many half-clad young women pranced across the screen. On one video a young guy with a mike was outdoors surrounded by four girls in bikinis. He was wearing a jacket, so it couldn't have been very warm. The girls must have been freezing and embarrassed, but not embarrassed enough to leave.

"Don't perm my bangs," I begged Peter. "I need them to cover up my forehead."

"Nonsense!" And he rolled my bangs up in curlers. I thought of leaving. But maybe Peter could change the bones in my face. Maybe he *did* know something I didn't. I grabbed hold of some impossible idea of beauty for myself, and glued by vanity, I stayed stuck in the chair.

"My customers are *always* happy," bragged Peter. "I have twelve new ones this month alone. I'm a lucky man. I get to play with the hair of lovely women, watch T.V., and get paid for it." It sounded like a terrible way to spend time.

Many video images later, Peter unrolled the perm. I swiveled the chair around to see myself, and he instantly swiveled it back.

"This is terrible! Oh no!" I frantically jumped out of my seat. I looked *terrible* in curls.

"I have to cut now," explained Peter, pushing me down in the chair.

"I *don't want* you to cut!"

"Be a good girl now," he said.

"I didn't come here to be a good girl. I came here to get my hair done."

He started cutting.

"What are you doing?"

He would not answer.

"Can you just tell me what you are doing?"

He snipped away. I took a deep breath and tried again. "Peter . . . don't cut the top, please."

His fingers worked in a mad rush.

"Peter!" Now I jumped up from the chair and threw the cape on the floor.

He went crazy. "You are impossible! Sit back down! I haven't combed it out yet!"

But I bolted into the ladies room, where I stuck my hair under the faucet. I wrapped a towel around my head, threw my money down, and ran home. The truth was I was going to look my worst tonight.

I had a bigger nose, a stranger chin, an uglier forehead, and smaller eyes; my face stuck out where it shouldn't. All the wrong things were big and all the right things were small.

I had to think about the way people said "trust me." It was a cheap way to get control. Trust was delicate—it was earned, intuited. It had to be guarded and meted out carefully, and when you were out of it you could not simply buy more. If you invested it wisely, however, it would grow. I had to close my trust account for now.

I dashed up the stairs and into the bathroom before my mother could say "how'd it go?" I restyled my hair over and over until I gave up. Then I tied it behind me in a ponytail and rigged an enormous bow. It was frizzy and wild, but my face went back to looking like the one I was used to.

By the time I'd decided not to spend the evening planning revenge on Peter and actually go to Michelle's party after all, it was six o'clock. Launching a missile had to be easier than getting myself together. There were so many things a female could do to enhance herself, and I was furiously doing all of them: Painting toenails (as if you could make someone fall in love with you because you chose "Tawny Peach" instead of "Italian Wine"). Curling hair, then un-curling it. Having a facial, tweezing eyebrows, rubbing in body oil, flossing teeth, and applying makeup. I had never spent much time doing these activities, yet they all seemed deeply familiar. As Gracie said, in the collective uncon-scious I'd probably been doing them for over seven million years. The perfume, the makeup base—recorded history was only ten thousand years old but rouge was probably older.

Anxiously, I looked through the Simone de Beauvoir book to see if she had subjected herself to anything like this. No, she had not betrayed herself even when hopelessly in love. I was on my own with all these fixings.

I went to borrow stockings from my mother.

"Don't open any new ones," she warned.

I dove into her drawer. I wanted light, sheer stockings. But the lightest, sheerest ones were in a brand-new package. She came in just as I was about to make off with them.

"You can't have those." She snatched them away from me.

"Ma . . ."

"Don't 'Ma' me."

"You don't want me to look good, do you?"

"Nan, what's the big deal?" My father had yanked the new stockings from her and was handing them to me. She rescued them out of his hand.

"The big deal is they're mine."

"It's just stockings, for Chrissakes," he boomed.

"Forget it, both of you," I said.

"I'm on *your* side," my father yelled.

"That's the trouble," said my mother.

"You won't let me on *your* side," he sneered at her.

"How would you know, you haven't been on my side for years."

"Damn!"

"I'm trying to go to a party and to have a good time," I screeched, and the door slammed.

"Good time," echoed my mother.

Then another door slammed and my father left the house.

How could Mr. Price ever fall for me now? Trouble would be written all over my face like graffiti.

Suddenly, I pulled all the clips out of my hair and washed off my makeup. Why bother going when I could stay home and read and find a way to understand this universe? I opened the de Beauvoir book. The words were meaningless; even the underlined paragraphs didn't make any sense. My mind was beyond logic. I unzipped my dress, threw off my shoes, and turned to a new chapter. But for once, the sentences in front of me couldn't put me in another place. I slammed the book closed and tried to hear some wisdom from within. Within was silent. And for a few minutes, I went the only place I could go: to sleep.

Then, a knock on my door.

My father stood there with a small package. "I don't know if they're fancy enough, but I got mediums from the store on the corner." He winked at me. "Hey, shouldn't you be dressed?"

I couldn't believe it—he handed me five new pairs of stockings. I opened up one of them and put them on. I stepped into the scarlet dress and began reconstruction work on my hair. I tried to elevate my mood along with the radio. It took several knocks for me to hear that someone was at the door again. "It's me," my mother said, and handed me the very stockings she had grabbed away. I lunged forward with a hug, but she didn't go for big sloppy emotions. She slipped away as soon as she could. I took off the new stockings and put on hers. Then I went to the mirror.

I closed my eyes and took a deep breath. And when I opened them, I couldn't believe what I saw: an almost beautiful girl.

"See, I *knew* you could do it!" Michelle looked me up and down, and grinned.

I gave Michelle her present—a beautiful scarf with sequins and rhinestones. Then I went to get a Coke. Bruce Tailor smiled and I smiled back, filled up a glass, and went to stand in between the speakers so nobody could talk to me. I was too nervous to do anything else. Anyway, I wanted to get a look at the party. Susan Seymour was dancing with her boyfriend, who was a senior and looked like he'd already been in contact with the CIA about a job. She looked happy and very orange in a jumpsuit. Ira was wearing a navy tuxedo with a purple shirt and a green glitter earring. Peter Druz draped himself over a chair like in a magazine ad, knowing people looked at him, and Darlene had gotten her hair bleached. Rosanna wasn't here yet.

Art was talking to Michelle's cousin, and Michelle's face told me she didn't like it. Her cousin had a long braid down her back, the kind of detail a lot of boys flip over.

"I can't believe it—it's not even real," Michelle shouted to me between the speakers.

"*What's* not real?" I shouted back.

"*Shhhshh!* Lora Lynn's braid. It's phony. And so is her interest in Art's father. That's all he talks about since we started reading that book. It's depressing." After making a face, Michelle went off to find someone a bottle opener.

Bruce Tailor made a motion for me to dance with him. I nodded okay, since I couldn't stand between the speakers all night and, anyway, my ears were starting to hurt.

He was wearing some kind of after-shave and a tie. His hands were cold but his feet moved fast and in rhythm. We danced together—I didn't want to have fun with Bruce, though; that wasn't my plan. "You look very nice." His brown eyes flickered.

"Thanks."

"Parties are strange, don't you think? I mean, I'm not really much of a party animal."

Then there was a slow dance and Bruce pulled me toward him and just for a second I tried to tell myself that it was Bruce who made my heart go crazy, and that his skin and his body would fill me up. I breathed in his after-shave and let him pull me even closer.

"What do you do for fun?" I asked.

"I play the clarinet. And I like gymnastics."

His hands were shaking, and I realized this was really an effort. I smiled. Bruce was a nice guy—sincere and not a jerk.

Then the door opened and Rosanna, wearing a maroon velvet antique dress, walked in. The velvet was so soft and full of color you just instantly wanted to put your hands all over it. Her cheeks picked up the tint and glowed warm and rosy, and her eyes were dark like something out of a portrait painting. Her fine black hair fell against the velvet, and the dress dipped in front to show her cleavage.

"She's a twelve," whispered Ira to Bruce, "and I used to hate math."

Rosanna walked up to Michelle and handed her a record album. She shook her hair and smiled at no one in particular. Four boys instantly fell in love.

Bruce didn't seem notice her. Out loud I thanked him for the dance, and to myself I thanked him for not drooling over Rosanna.

"What do you think of Mr. Price?" asked Bruce, still dancing.

"He's okay."

"Michelle, do you have any scotch?" Rosanna walked

over to the beverages. There were only punch and soft drinks, but Rosanna hunted under the bar and came up with a bottle of whiskey that she generously poured into a Coke. She gulped it all down and poured another. I was flabbergasted. After two or three of those concoctions Rosanna started giggling.

I let Bruce hold me, and I felt his back, which had plenty of lean muscles. I had to admit it was nice to be held, to have a boy pay attention, and to feel how kind he was. I relaxed in his arms and I was tempted to tell him about the stockings in a funny way to make him laugh.

Then Rowland Price opened the door and stood there looking around. I tried to steer Bruce around so I could see him, but Bruce didn't cooperate. Then Mr. Price pushed his hand through his hair and sauntered in with a bemused look on his face. He was wearing brown leather pants and a sports jacket. When Mr. Price stood there, he melted down Bruce and everyone else into insignificant young kids. He waved to a couple of people. Then he smiled my way and I tried to untangle myself from Bruce, but I didn't want to act like a fool, and Bruce was too involved in dancing to realize I was trying to get free. Anyway, I sort of liked dancing with him.

Meanwhile, Mr. Price gave Michelle a present, and munched on pretzels. I scanned the place for Rosanna. She wasn't around. Finally the dance ended. I found the courage to leave Bruce and walk up to Mr. Price. Brazenly, I asked him to dance. Why not? It was a party, right?, and the music was loud! Then I was dancing with *him!*

I let the slit in my dress shift around freely. Otherwise why had I bothered buying a sexy dress? He laughed, trying to keep up with me. But seeing him moving right opposite me was enough inspiration for me to become the principal dancer in the Bolshoi Ballet.

I moved and shimmied, grabbing onto the beat and pushing the rhythm out of every muscle I had. Every time I did a fancy move, Mr. Price would raise his eyebrows to show he was impressed, then try to equal it. He was even more beautiful moving, because he was a little shy and that seemed so sweet and lovely. Who would have guessed? I danced in a frenzy. At one point I dropped down, and using the slit in my dress, I actually managed a split. I leaped up again like I'd been thrown out of a molten volcano. I would have danced on the ceiling if I could have figured out how to beat gravity. The drumbeat felt like it was in my solar plexus, and I gave myself over to it. Arms waving, head turning, my torso like a whip, no place in my body was still. My adrenaline kept my energy high right to the last bar of the song. By now everyone was watching. When it ended I was huffing and puffing so hard I could hardly realize the intensity in Mr. Price's voice when he said that one simple word.

"ROSANNA."

She had been clapping and shrieking encouragement along with everyone else. That's really all I knew, because Bruce Tailor walked me over to a folding chair, and when I looked up from sipping the Coke he gave me, Mr. Price was gone.

Chapter Eleven

Nobody had to tell me that they were together.

She had vanished also, hadn't she? What had Mr. Price thought as I worked myself up on the dance floor in a frenzy? That I was funny or pathetic? Or worse, was he totally distracted, thinking only of Rosanna?

In my scarlet dress that Michelle thought was a knockout and my father thought was sexy, I had simply been the commercial until the real program came on.

Humiliation and disappointment pulled me down and made me motionless. I would try my father's solution. I guzzled down the sickly-sweet spiked punch. Maybe I could reach that state where nothing bothered me. Maybe I had a future as an alcoholic. Six glasses of punch would certainly provide the answer.

For five minutes I felt painless euphoria. People spun by and my body grew light. I danced without a partner. Mr. Price. How nice it would be to tongue kiss someone, I decided. Anyone. Suddenly I felt friendly. Where were Bruce's lips? They might come in very handy. I looked around for him and even called out his name.

"B—e—rr—uuuuoooo—ce!"

I will never know if he came over to me, because I went unconscious. The first thing I saw when I came to was the bottom of Michelle's toilet bowl and a pair of high-heeled shoes that belonged to a voice that was asking, "Are you okay?"

This struck me as a hilarious question, so I laughed. Big mistake. My head hurt and the world was wrapped in cotton. Michelle got me up, steered me to her bedroom, and locked the door. It was only ten forty-five, but that was the last of the party for me. In the morning Michelle's mother made us coffee, and I groaned about making a fool of myself.

"It sort of rounds out your image," said Michelle.

"People liked seeing me act like a jerk?"

"The word is 'loved.' Your feminist rhetoric was getting on everyone's nerves. Anyway, there was a bigger scandal!"

I had gulped down those drinks so I could erase the truth from my mind, but here was another day and the truth had come back to zing me between the eyes. Truth was a crackerjack marksman.

"Mr. Price and Rosanna!" said Michelle, but I already had tasted that thought in my mind. I guess I wasn't an alcoholic, because hearing that news didn't make me want to drink. It made me want to go back to sleep. But I had already slept ten hours.

When I got home just before noon, Buster was throwing shirts and socks into a satchel. "I'm going to Europe on business." He seemed happy and preoccupied.

"But it's Saturday. I thought you were leaving next Wednesday."

"I switched the trip around. I think your mother needs a little space from me."

It seemed my mother and he had a galaxy of space between them already and were orbiting different suns.

"Paris, Rome, and a quick stop in Barcelona. We're buying a company there."

Paris, Rome, and a quick stop at the mistress's, I thought.

"Be back in six days," he said. He looked up for a minute. "Sometime I'd like to take you."

"Me and Mom," I corrected him.

"Here, write down your sizes." He handed me a piece of paper.

What would happen if he found someone? Would he get a divorce? Would he just takes lots of trips? Or maybe I was missing the point. Maybe he already had another woman.

Nan and I dropped Buster at the airport, and the car was as silent as a meditation room. Each of us was locked in her own thoughts, and to speak those thoughts would only be fuel for pain. I had brought along my books, and I leafed through the pages as she drove us home, even though reading in a car makes me dizzy.

"I just want you to know I went through this book stage too," said my mother.

"What happened?"

"Life. And it wasn't in books."

"But life *is* in books! Books inspire you to think, and then with an open mind you can gain perspective."

"I thought I was giving birth to a daughter, but instead I gave birth to a library. Who's the boy this is all about? Do I know him?"

"No." My mind raced, trying to think of a way to sound totally normal. "It's just the usual unrequited love."

"I know the feeling." She half smiled at me.

Suddenly I felt a surge of sorrow and a wave of protection toward her. "Maybe we can do some interesting stuff together while Dad is gone," I said.

"A movie? Shopping?"

She had great taste, elegance when she wanted, but clothes don't make you happy unless you have somewhere to wear them.

"Try again."

"Okay, this is a game. You want to throw pots with me?"

"Maybe."

"I know what you want. You want night classes and things full of purpose from me, don't you? Well, I advise you to take the movie."

Which is where we went Saturday night. I looked around to check out if Mr. Price was there. I wished I could hate him now, and maybe I did, but still my head turned nervously everywhere we went. I checked all the streets, and the deli afterward. I shuddered to think where he really was.

"Unrequited love?" my mother asked. "Poor girl." And she actually slipped her hand into mine.

Chapter Twelve

On Monday new paintings hung in the hallways of the Center. They were so sincere and so awkward and ever so slightly improved from the last batch, they softened my heart. I walked into the sewing room smiling.

Maria's fingers moved rapidly in an intricate dance. "I don't know why I'm even doing this," she sighed, and took a minute to push back her blond streak of hair.

"It's because she's a bully." May, also knitting a square for the afghan, nodded toward Gracie.

Gracie hummed as she sewed together the blanket from the wild assortment of dazzling squares. "This is more important than making yourself another skirt," she said to Ruth. "We need to make a statement for peace."

"I made statements my whole life. Nobody listened," said Ruth.

"Now that you're seventy, they're going to listen," said Maria. "Right, Gracie?"

I wondered why I had managed to fall in with a bunch of potentially radical old ladies. Had Mr. Price been here, or was it just fate?

"I did for others my whole life, thank you very much, and it got me a son who lives in New Mexico, and a husband who's at the racetrack." Ruth operated a sewing machine as if it were a government weapon. "Personally speaking, I'd rather have a new skirt."

"Eventually you'll help us," said Gracie philosophically. "Deep down, everyone in the world wants peace. Even you."

Ruth clucked at her.

"Gracie says we gave birth to a generation of folks who are trashing this planet, and since we're the mothers we ought to have our say." May turned the thought over in her mind and found it interesting.

"What do you think, young lady?" Gracie turned to me.

What I thought was not worth repeating—that political thought was not going to change my life. After all, Mr. Price had vanished with Rosanna, hadn't he, without a political thought in his head. Maybe I was deluding myself. Maybe what I thought was important was wrong. Or irrelevant. But I didn't say that. Instead I said, "My generation isn't capable of fixing the mess it took hundreds of years to create."

"Correct. We can't expect your generation to succeed without a lot of help." said Gracie. "The way I see it, the people in their middle years are too caught up with making money and worrying about their families to do very much. It's going to take my generation to mobilize the others. Especially the women. That's the reason for this afghan. Do you know how to knit?" Gracie held out a ball of yarn in my direction.

I should have been happy hearing her hopes were so firm and solid, but I was miserable. "Maybe this afghan is going to be useless. After all, one lousy afghan is not a lot in the scheme of things," I said.

"That's what we all used to say," said Ruth, "but I'm surprised at *you,* Brogan."

"This afghan is about the common person making a commitment to step outside his own immediate sphere of personal concern," said Gracie.

"But the common person needs someone to lead the way," I countered. "That's how we can become great, from our teachers."

"That's not how I see it," said Gracie.

"But even you, you're someone special," I said.

"I'm *not* special," Gracie said, almost yelling. "I just want to *do* something. The solution is going to come from all people!"

"I doubt it," I said.

"I don't," said Gracie.

"What makes you so certain of everything? To make changes you have to be flexible!"

"I *am* flexible," shouted Gracie. "When I hear a really *good* idea, my flexibility kicks right in. You remind me of someone, I'm sad to say," she said.

"Maybe you should just stick to making dresses. That's what I'm supposed to be helping you do, make dresses, not this stupid afghan. Ames wouldn't like it, spending government funds illegally."

"So it's easy to say you want a better world, but when it comes down to buckling down and working for it, the minute you don't get your own way, you quit."

I wasn't quitting, I was just mad. Thinking all the humanistic thoughts in the world didn't make Mr. Price fall in love with me, did it? "I have to do what Ames wants."

"Another Janie," sighed Gracie.

"What does *that* mean?" I asked. "I'm not another *anyone*!"

"She won't talk about it," hinted Maria. "It's a sore spot."

"I can talk plenty," said Gracie, not looking up. "I have a daughter who's just as spoiled and self-absorbed as you are. I raised her to see the world's problems as her own. She took all the right courses, we had all the right discussions, and *still* she thinks she can hide in her own little nest. Enough said!"

"I'm *not* hiding! And I'm nothing *like* your daughter. What do you think I'm *doing* here—trying to see more about life *right here*! At first I hated it and I didn't even want to stay, but I did." I twisted the yarn out of shape.

"So you did us a favor and you stayed?" Gracie asked.

"I stayed because I wanted to."

Maybe I was angry with Gracie for making me think there was hope. But there was only America going down the drain. There were only parents like mine, and teachers like Mr. Price who fell in love with someone because she was beautiful, while he forced you to read books about being real.

"I am here to do my job," I shouted much too loudly. "So, now, what kind of dress will you be making for the fashion show, Gracie?" I said, meanness swelling up in me and bursting out, meanness I didn't even know was there. "A peace-march outfit, perhaps?"

Gracie answered without any anger, "I'll have to think about it."

Thoughtful . . . no, ashamed, I sat on the bus. So sick, turning on Gracie. It was an evil part of me that wanted to crush another person—the part of me that had been crushed. "She was not following the rules. You were right," I told myself. It was a lie. But as the bus lugged itself through the streets like a great exhausted beast, the lies kept coming. I became hard with righteousness. I had asserted myself. I could not worry the big worries anymore. I had to worry about losing Mr. Price to Rosanna. I had to join with May and make skirts if I wanted to win in life. But I could sew hundreds of skirts, all perfectly, and my face would still never look like Rosanna's. God had already sewn my face. All I could do was to make my insides pretty, and right now that seemed hopeless.

Michelle furiously passed me a note first thing Tuesday morning. I couldn't open it right away because Mr. Price was on my aisle. Michelle squeaked impatiently from two rows over, so finally I unfolded it and read the tiny handwriting:

"Art broke up with me!"

Michelle wasn't wearing any makeup and her clothes were a wreck. She probably was delirious with dread. She thought her life was over. In the past that would have lasted for at least ten or fifteen minutes and then she'd have had a hard and long recovery of about an hour, in which time she would have found herself another boyfriend.

But that was before she'd ever slept with anyone.

Michelle needed educating as much as I did. I made a vow: I would try to arm her with theories, insights, facts, and observations. If she'd let me.

But I was the person who had just come down on Gracie for being truly independent. Where did I stand, and how could I help anyone?

Chapter Thirteen

Michelle sniffled so noisily on the way home that I had to ask *the* question: "Why did he break up with you?"

"Are you going to give me a theory or be a real person?" Michelle paused, and looked straight ahead in her most dramatic fashion.

"I'll be a person."

Michelle shuffled her feet. "Remember when you and I knew everything the other person was thinking?" she asked.

"Yep. But we're older and more complex now, so you've got to tell me. Come on."

"He said, 'Michelle, you're happy. I'm not.' "

"That was *it*?"

"Stupid me—I thought I was supposed to be happy."

"Depends on *why* you're happy."

"What is *that* supposed to mean?"

"You can be happy lots of ways. Fulfilling ways or cheap ones."

"I knew it! Get lost, Brogan."

"Okay, okay, let me try again. Look, Art's father is a veteran struggling with a lot of problems. Does Art ever talk about that?"

"No. But I'm not going *out* with his *father*."

"That's not what I mean, Michelle."

"So maybe I'm not deep, okay. But at least I'm not a manhater."

"I'm *not* a manhater!"

"Yes, you are. Except for one man. You think it's a secret? Well it's not, because nonsearching me figured it out. You're totally bonkers over Mr. Price. Everyone knows it. Why don't you admit it? Then at least we could talk!"

"I thought you wanted to talk about *you.*"

"Except I don't know who I'm talking to anymore," said Michelle. "You don't tell me stuff."

"I'm going home," I told Michelle, and turned and walked away with what I hoped was dignity but felt more akin to despair.

My mother was in a PBS-documentary mode. When she settled in at three thirty P.M. it meant she was on a downslide.

"Hi," she called out, her voice raspy and nasal. I walked into the den.

"Oh, Brogan, this was *so* moving! Martin Luther King! Oh God, why do all the great leaders get killed?"

"Maybe so other leaders can take their place."

"As if *anybody* could take his place."

"Mom, leaders or not, we all have to fight our own battles."

"*Ssshhh!* Listen to that speech: free at last. That's what I'd like to be."

"I hate it when you make it sound like you want to die. So *do* something about it."

"Don't yell at me, Brogan."

I hated it when I yelled, but it was because she seemed so pathetic. "Mom, you have all your arms, legs, eyes. There's nothing wrong with you. You just have to fight for what you want."

She sulked, so I shut up and made a pot of chamomile tea. For the ten thousandth time I told her how inspiring she was to me because she'd been active early in the Civil Rights movement on the college campuses and then later in the women's movement. She had fought discrimination in the schools by breaking white picket lines and teaching in black neighborhoods. But she said I was the strong one in the family.

I didn't tell her I had to be strong because every time I saw her weak I got scared. It was like someone had emptied the gas right out of her tank. She stepped on the pedal to drive and stalled. I wanted to find a way to replenish the gas but I didn't know how.

The King coverage went on and on. My mother was so moved she burst out sobbing. "See, there *are* some good people," she moaned.

"I *know!*" And even though I'd acted hideously to Gracie, was checkmate with Mr. Price, had alienated Michelle, and didn't trust my father, I did know.

The week was quiet with no Buster around to provoke things. Finally, Nan went back to throwing pots, and we made stir-fry dinners and watched movies on television. Nan went crazy over certain actresses. She either loved them or raged at them, and tried to get me to agree with her extreme opinions. I couldn't understand feeling that strongly about a movie, so I stayed in my room reading, trying to formulate what I would finally write for Price's class.

Nan would yell out, "Want to see Ronald Coleman in an incredible film?"

"No thanks." So many ideas jiggled in my mind, hollering for order, there was a stampede instead of a lineup. "Not tonight. But maybe we could talk . . ."

Of course I liked movies, but I was busy working out a puzzle. Everything seemed connected, but what in our culture caused what? Was it industrialization, technology, and the corporate mentality that caused competition, robotlike materialism, and greed? Or were we already off-balance as a species because women had been second-class citizens way before the cotton gin was ever invented? And what had to change?

"Talk!" said Nan. "You mean more theories?!"

When the movie was over, she made us tea. "Okay, what do you want to talk about?"

"Reich," I said.

"Reich?" She groaned.

"I thought you might be interested because he wrote about the early sixties and the transformation in consciousness."

"The sixties were great," smiled Nan. "I thought I knew who I was then. Unfortunately I only knew what I was *against.* It's so much harder to be *for* things, you know?"

"Maybe that's why Reich's heroes have since gotten jobs on Wall Street, died, or lived off their reputations. After all the alternative life-styles, the marches, the communes, Vietnam, and the psychedelic drugs, what's been accomplished? Even racism has returned!"

"Women. In the sixties we realized we had to do it for ourselves. We found out we couldn't tell men to do it for us, then complain that we had no power. That hasn't changed. Even I know it, Brogan, I really do."

I couldn't believe it!

Then the phone rang. It was Bruce Tailor. My mom laughed when I told her I'd take it in my room.

"Just wondering—why did you call my name at Michelle's party before you passed out?"

I wasn't about to admit to Bruce Tailor that while I was drunk I had temporarily searched for his lips. "Did I really call your name?"

"Well, I thought you did," he said regretfully, and hung up.

Later I did remember something, although it wasn't about Michelle's party. It was the Friday gym inspection that we'd been told about last week. Pat Stone had picked me for her team, which meant I'd qualify for interschool volleyball. Even if Reich didn't approve of competition, I wanted a try at playing state-of-the-art volleyball—sweating, hitting, jumping, and fighting in the heat of battle; pummeling the ball, using strategy, wanting to win. My private theory was that it was good for girls; furthermore, I liked it. However, that meant getting my filthy sneakers out of my locker Thursday evening and putting them into the washing machine before gym class.

Since I didn't want to carry my sneakers around all day, I decided to get them after school. To reach the girls' locker room I had to go through the big airy gym. There were large windows on three sides, and the late-afternoon light was quite ethereal in there, at least on that day. It was empty and quite grand. Hard to believe this was the room where I'd heard violent disagreements over where a ball had bounced and if a foul had been committed. Hard to picture the sweat and the intensity while the dim, diffuse light lit it up like a cathedral.

I was heading for the locker room when I noticed a body at the far end silently and elegantly turning on the high bar. He was working with great concentration, so he didn't notice me. Whoever it was had a long muscular body, beautifully formed thighs and calves, and a perfect torso. He twirled around the bar, his legs extended then tucked in. Pausing almost at the top in spectacular control, he went around again, and finally in an awesome twist he exchanged hands and it looked as if he were flying in the air, defying gravity. But he didn't stop there. It was as if this boy had found a way to cheat the laws of physics. He flew around the bar with his chest arched, his legs extended, and his arms taut, and it was no more bothersome or cumbersome to him than the floor was to Baryshnikov. *Swish,* went his body, and I was stranded midway in admiration. Then he did an upside-down split at the very top of the bar, let go and flew, really flew off the thing—but not before he'd executed a midair somersault and a flip—and he landed on the ground like a surprise. I tiptoed out of there, thinking this performance would remain an eternal mystery to me unless someday in the future I watched a competition and was able to pick him out.

Just as I got to the girls' locker-room door, he turned to get a towel. The face that belonged to that incredible body was Bruce Tailor's.

Chapter Fourteen

Buster was due home Friday night. My mother went into action. She got her hair colored and permed, and her nails, which usually looked like they belonged to a miner, actually got polished. As if that would change anything.

And then, at seven thirteen exactly, he was back.

Even though he was suffering from jet lag, Buster seemed cheered to see us both at the airport and insisted we go to dinner. Chez Tin Tin was a place my parents saved for special occasions, so I got my hopes up that this would be one of them. If I could have prayed right there over the poppy seed rolls and the pink tablecloth that our family would make a sudden tilt toward happiness, I would have been eloquent.

Next time he went abroad, he would have to take us,

Buster was saying. You needed your family there because although Paris was beautiful, the French were awful. They made fun of his accent and were difficult and superior. Meanwhile, I kept listening for clues of what else might have happened.

I ordered roast beef and took a tiny sip of my mother's wine. While my father filled my mother in on some of the details—when he wanted to he could be a real storyteller—my mind started to embroider the scene: Buster would stop drinking. The three of us would go to the theater together, take hikes, and best of all, when we were all together at home we'd sit around the dinner table and talk like a real family and feel close. These kinds of imaginings were old stuff for me. I had long given them up, and it was just the momentary lightness at the table that brought them back in such force. They had been crossed out in my mind with a big "X" years ago, right next to the space labeled "happy family."

Before dessert my mother excused herself and went to the ladies' room. She was wearing a red dress and heels. Her efforts had paid off. She looked great.

My father leaned over to me. "It wasn't quite like I had planned."

"Was it better or worse?"

"Worse."

"That's too bad."

"You're telling me," he said, missing my sarcasm.

Nan returned with fresh lipstick, looking bright and almost happy. She even smiled at Buster when she sat down. Maybe he'd been right when he'd said they needed a little space from each other. Maybe now that he'd gotten this trip out of his system, and not found a mistress, he would make an effort at home. I worked on my theories silently.

"Presents!" he announced. Out of his trench coat he brought two packages. He handed me a biggish one and my mother the other, which was much smaller. Perhaps hers was jewelry. Perhaps he really was getting a grip on himself.

I opened up my package to find a black beaded bag that was incredibly decorated and very expensive-looking. Nan oohed and aahhed, and I did the same. I gave Buster a kiss.

Then my mother opened up her little package, taking a long time. She wasn't used to presents from Buster. I was as curious as she was, thinking how one small gift could change everything.

"Perfume," she said.

"Do you like it?"

Buster gave perfume to his secretary, his mother-in-law, his sister, and every other woman he knew. I had to wonder why he would get me something so grown-up and her something so impersonal.

Nan put the perfume in her bag, and ordered a decaf.

Later, I told her Buster must have made a mistake, and I offered her the bag. She asked me if I had theories about why she had received perfume instead of a real gift. I said I didn't have a theory.

I couldn't sleep for the fighting. Buster yelled he couldn't do anything right. He'd bought her a present, hadn't he? What did she want, diamonds?

Nan screamed back. "You undermine me every chance you get!" She said she didn't understand what was happening.

Buster had gone to Paris and hadn't been able to fool around. My mother didn't know what was bothering him. I knew and couldn't say.

Tomorrow, Saturday, I would go to the Center and apologize to Gracie. I would tell her about my parents. She would give me advice, fill me with hope like she filled her friends. When I left there I'd know what to do.

The next day I got up at eight. I wanted to be gone from the house all day if possible. I was out of the house at nine. Someone came reeling toward me on a ten-speed bike. I didn't want to be slowed down.

"I didn't know you lived on this street. We live right down the block!" Bruce Tailor, wearing a down jacket and skull cap, gave me a red-cheeked grin.

"Morning," I said, feeling caught. He seemed so normal, so upbeat, so boyish.

"Want to get some breakfast?"

"Oh! Can't, Bruce. It's my mother's birthday, and I have to get her a present. And then I have to catch a bus. I'm doing some work for class."

"Want some company? Things are quiet at my house. Too quiet."

"Too quiet?"

"My uncle."

"Oh," I said, as if I understood.

"He's very sick."

Then I remembered. The asbestos poisoning. I felt stupid. "I'm so sorry, Bruce."

"It's awful." He looked away for a minute. "My father is going to pieces. They're twins." Then he smiled. "That's why I could use a change of pace."

I didn't know anything about death. "It must be terrible," I said, feeling horribly inadequate. "I know what you mean about a change of pace, though."

"I'm going to the Hayden Planetarium. Did you know, if our solar system could fit into a cup, our galaxy would be as large as all of North America?"

"You find out stuff like that in the planetarium?"

"Come with me," said Bruce.

The morning was so bright, and so was Bruce's smile, that I wished it were just another morning and I were from just another family and didn't have to see anyone about anything. But I wasn't. "I really have to see this person," I said. "Alone."

"Too bad," said Bruce. "On the wall they have this great diagram. It shows you how it would take four point three light years to reach Alpha Centauri, which is over twenty-four trillion miles away. Isn't that amazing?" Bruce hopped on his bike.

I wanted to call to him to tell him to take me to another universe where I'd wake up in a different galaxy, but Bruce had pedaled away, and anyway, there was only this universe and I had to catch a bus.

Chapter Fifteen

I bought my mother a beautiful silk scarf hoping it would do the trick. She got emotional on her birthday, and often she sounded more like a caller on a radio talk show than someone celebrating a year of life. Every year I hoped it would go better; every year I tried to give better and better presents. But my presents weren't enough to make the difference, and even as I forked over all my savings I knew that.

As I rounded the corner to the Center, I could see it was more active than during the week. There were some people boarding a bus, and the front hallway was almost crowded. I had never been here on a weekend, so I didn't know what to expect. I would go to Ames's office to tell him I was putting in extra time.

His door was closed. He didn't work Saturdays! Maybe the sewing room wouldn't be open either. I'd only been aware of my small schedule. I bounded up the stairs and hurried down the hallway and into the room.

"Well!" May put down her knitting and gave me a big hug. "She's here on a Saturday yet! So you like us!" she said, and gave me the elbow. "I can understand that. We're nice people, aren't we, Ruth?"

"Some of us are nice, some of us are just old," said Ruth. "Me, I'm just old."

I figured Ruth wanted some attention, so I gave her a hug too.

"Okay, okay, so maybe I'm a little nice too. What I really am is crazy, though. Can you believe this?" She held up what she was working on. It was an afghan square. "Just one, for Gracie's campaign. She shamed me into it. Isn't it pretty?" It had maroon and turquoise yarns.

"It's beautiful. So when does Gracie get here?"

May shook her head. "She doesn't come in on Saturdays."

I picked up my bag to leave.

"You know, Gracie hasn't been here all week. She said not to expect her."

"*What?*"

"She said she'd be back when she'd collected five hundred squares for her afghan," said Ruth.

"Isn't she something?" said May.

"Did she leave because of me?" I wondered out loud.

Ruth shrugged. "Don't know, sweetheart. We only see

Gracie here, like you do, weekday afternoons. Can we help you, dear?"

"No thanks. . . . Uh, see you next Thursday." Propelled by anxiety, I ran out.

Gracie was somewhere doing something. I just had to concentrate and I would find her. Then we would sit down over a cup of tea and I would explain everything. She would laugh and tell me how it all was going to change.

Downstairs, I looked up Gracie's last name—Pevsner—in the phone book and found her address.

"I'm glad I caught you," said Ruth, rushing downstairs. She handed me a piece of paper with an announcement of a "Grandmas for Peace Campaign." "I tried to call after you but you were too fast for me."

I grabbed the paper, which said there was a meeting right then at the Greater Mercury Savings Bank. This time I managed to yell "thanks" before I bolted.

I never was good with apologies spoken in sentences, so on the way to the bank I bought a small cake in a buttery-smelling bakery to give to Gracie as an offering. The chocolate kept me company on the bus ride across the park.

I had to hold it carefully as I squeezed between the many bodies crowding the Greater Mercury Savings Bank. About fifty people sat in folding chairs, while others stood around. Up at the officer's desk, wearing her bright-blue eye shadow and trusty peace pin, Gracie talked into a microphone, explaining that seniors had to carry the burden for world peace because everyone else was too damned busy.

"But look at us," said one woman with thick glasses and

thick legs, "we're Republicans, Democrats, and old farts in here. We could never work together."

"We can make a unified statement. That we feel responsible. That we are concerned. That we have a contribution to make." Gracie's voice was confident.

"I'm too tired to contribute," said another woman, who held a cane.

"You work for this, you won't be tired."

"What a nerve," whispered the lady with the cane.

That's when Gracie got someone to help her and she unfolded a hand-painted banner that read:

GRANDMAS FOR PEACE—AFGHAN CAMPAIGN.

"I like that," said one man. " 'Grandmas for Peace.' My wife is one of those."

"So if you want to knit for peace, sign here," said Gracie. "We'll start in New York State, then go on to Pennsylvania!" She had paper and pens, and right away people started to line up.

I stood there amazed. If Mr. Price could see this, he would have to tear up all the theories in *The Greening of America* about the new generation being the cure for the nation's problems and the older people having just given up. Gracie was beyond the analysis of the social scientists.

"Why you doing this?" challenged one man. "To get your picture in the paper?"

"Since we don't have to worry about being elected, we have an incredible luxury—our desires are pure."

"Pure bullshit," the man said.

But Gracie had won the crowd.

"Shshhh! You rude man. *I* want to hear this." The woman with the cane got up and headed for the line.

I got on line too. It moved slowly. I rehearsed what I would say when I finally reached Gracie. How much I admired her. What a mistake I had made. How now I realized she was the person to help me. When I reached the list, though, I simply took the pen and signed.

"Well, well, well."

"Hello, Gracie."

Chapter Sixteen

At about four thirty Gracie said, "Let's go, I'm hungry. Don't trust people who never get hungry."

We made our way to the bus stop just as the bus had pulled away. "If it was good enough for Golda Meir to eat at home after running a government, it's good enough for me." And she took off after the bus.

I thought she was crazy. Buses don't change their minds once they pull out. I jogged unenthusiastically behind.

"Come on," she yelled insistently. I picked up my pace and joined her.

"We'll never make it," I huffed, and grudgingly passed her.

"Make sure he can see you from his side window!"

As I was going to dash forward, the bus slowed down to

a stop. Completely out of breath, we boarded. Gracie thanked the driver, whom she knew, and paid for both of us. "I don't believe in giving up," she said as we sat down.

I handed Gracie the bakery bag.

"I bought you some cake. Gracie, you know so much. You care so much about everyone, even people you don't know." The light came in the window and etched Gracie's pale skin with lines I hadn't noticed before. I liked the lines. She lived up to the lines in her face—they were not extra things but necessary definitions. "And I was so stupid to you that day. It's just that sometimes it even hurts to admit that things could be better, because you get used to them being rotten. And if it's true they *could* be better, it means you really have to *do* something to make them better. You have to think about what that is, and then you actually have to act on it." I was out of breath from my own logic.

The moments passed, the bus lumbering along gracelessly while I sat there miserable and stupid. It wasn't like Gracie to be so quiet.

"Gracie?"

"Everything you say is true," she said.

"Then why do you look so strange?"

"Because."

"You're still mad at me?"

She laughed. "Of course not."

She was still mad, she had to be; otherwise why was she so quiet? I sighed.

"Brogan, I must tell you something. It is not something I'm proud of. But I don't want you to get the wrong idea about me. I'm nobody special."

"How many people are doing what you're doing? How many people—"

"Stop! Please." Gracie looked agitated. "You know so little about me. You are looking for a hero, and I am not a hero, young lady."

"But you are!"

"Brogan, I have a thirty-year-old daughter who is not talking to me."

"So what?"

"So what is it's a terrible thing, and I can't really blame her. There is more to me than you can imagine."

"Whatever it is, there's a reason for it, I know that."

"Yes," said Gracie with resignation, "there is a reason."

The bus dropped us off. Gracie and I walked to a grocery, where she picked out some onions and potatoes. Then I walked her home. It was getting cold, but she didn't seem to feel it. We went through the warm lobby and up to her apartment.

I looked around and saw pieces of her life. She had an upright piano, a small bedroom, and lots of artwork on the walls. She seemed to like oriental figures, and there was a wall full of books. There were pictures of Sol, and of her daughter at about my age.

She had a whole life I knew nothing about. I had thought of older people as just a collection of has-beens, as relics, if I thought of them at all. They were people who moved slowly, or didn't hear well, or couldn't understand anything. I had never thought of them as people with more stories to tell, more life under their belts. Or more problems.

Gracie cut up the onions, took out some bread, and

warmed up soup from the fridge. The apartment filled with a delicious aroma.

"So being that it's almost Saturday night, let me ask you a question. Do you have a boyfriend?"

"No."

"I met Sol when I was only a little older than you, nineteen."

"I don't want one," I said vehemently. "I have too many other things to think about. Gracie, my mother is forty-two years old. She doesn't know what to do in her life, and she thinks she's washed up."

"That's not a good reason not to have a boyfriend." She ladled the soup into two bowls.

"It's not the only reason."

"But you are concerned about your mother, yes?"

I nodded.

"Brogan, women have been taught to live for men. When we do, we develop an emptiness. That hole is what made women good workers—wives, mothers, secretaries—for *men*." She picked up a picture of her daughter and gazed at it. "But *not* leaders, not thinkers, not artists—except for the rare exception. Am I right?"

"I've said almost the same words," I told her. "Except about the emptiness. *I feel it,* Gracie!" I said, my voice shaky.

"Of course you do," she said calmly. "But you're going to get rid of that empty space. That's what I'm doing, Brogan. Getting rid of mine."

"*You* have it? *You* can't have it!"

She sighed. "Mine was big. Have some soup." She handed me my portion. "I only wish my daughter wanted to deal with hers instead of filling it up with shoes and earrings and dresses from the mall."

"Maybe those things fill it up."

"Only in a temporary, silly way." Gracie looked disgusted. "What a waste! There wasn't a rally she didn't go to, a reading she didn't hear, a gallery she didn't visit, a summer camp she didn't have the chance to enjoy—I tried to make her mind disquieted, seeking, curious. Instead, she turned out to care about manicures and waistlines. It's absurd."

It was ironic. "She has to find her own happiness," I said meekly, afraid of Gracie's passion.

"So they tell me!" She tore off a piece of bread. "Well, I heard she finally went to her first PTA meeting. Her oldest daughter, Robin, is ten. Maybe she'll get concerned about the school."

"It seems nobody is exactly the way we want them to be," I said, wanting to comfort Gracie.

"Exactly! Janie doesn't understand why I don't just take a cruise somewhere. She doesn't understand me at all."

"She must be proud of you."

"She *is* proud of me. I'm just not proud of her. But I am finished talking about it."

I waited for the bus for a long time. I'd never even told Gracie about my parents. For all their faults, Nan and Buster tolerated my ideas. They had never not loved me because of them. Janie Pevsner must have had a hard time because she was not radical enough for Gracie. Who ever thought *that* could happen?

I danced around in one spot to keep warm, and munched on a pretzel stick. Watching the streets get crowded with Saturday night activity, I realized that for once Mr. Price's face was not stamped in between my eyes like some indelible tatoo. Rosanna was not on my mind either. Gracie, who had dents of her own, had spoken to me like I was a grown-up. I was glad I was not her daughter but her friend.

In the freezing night air, I was in the world again directly and clearly. For once, my theories were suspended, my doubts were sleeping, and my hopes were high.

Chapter Seventeen

The T.V. was off even though it was prime time. Suspicions
of chocolate chip cookies led me into the kitchen. They
were cooling on a cookie sheet, but from the pottery wheel
downstairs I could hear Nan humming. Humming! I wondered if she was on drugs. Maybe she'd found a lover. Or
perhaps she'd kicked Buster out.

"Dad home?" I asked tentatively as I descended.

"Upstairs."

"You okay?" I'd seen so many T.V. movies where wild
mood swings can be the beginning of deep psychosis.

"Brogan, even though it's that day, I'm great!"

"You *are*?"

"Yes! Come look! A whole different direction."

I walked over to the wheel. But she wasn't using the
wheel. She had made a giant free-form clay piece.

"What is it, Mom?" I said, walking around it. Whatever it was it had force, vitality, and complexity. I liked it.

"Brogan, it was so much fun! So intense. I felt alive. What it is I don't know. It came out of me. I remembered all the nagging you've done, so I took my mood down here. Then these shapes began bursting out of me. Why did I think all these years that because I worked in clay, I had to make lamp bases and salad bowls?"

"I don't know, Ma. Here's your present." I ran to hug her.

Even before she opened it up she said, "Thanks for caring so much, Brogan."

Back in my room I pressed the button in my psyche that had Mr. Price's name on it. I was curious to see how strong the reaction would be. Would the ache pulse through me as always? So I whispered his name—deep in my solar plexus I felt the awful hunger still there. I wanted him. But there was caution next to the want.

I whispered his name and hugged the pillow. I kissed it, rubbed my lips against it, and moaned. Fires built but not as wildly.

They were at it. There was no dinner prepared. Nan said it was because it was her birthday and she thought they were going out. But naturally, Buster had forgotten. He'd been drinking and his mood wasn't very stable. He yelled he'd make it up to her tomorrow, could she please just make a couple of burgers. She yelled she hadn't been born tomorrow, she'd been born today, and he could make his own damn burger. Any other man would have remembered. Bought a lousy present. Planned to take his wife out.

"You want to go *out*?" Buster yelled. "Fine! Put on your coat, we'll go out."

He yelled up the stairs. "Did you hear that, Brogan, we're all going *out* for your mother's birthday. We'll have a real family night," he said menacingly.

When he was like this he reminded me of Jackie Gleason in the old *Honeymooners* reruns. Only he wasn't funny.

"Wear high-heeled shoes, a dress, lots of makeup—look your best," he advised. "I want to be proud of you." He didn't usually tell me what to wear. Could it be that he'd snapped to his senses and was going to take us somewhere extra nice?

Nan trudged upstairs. "I don't want to go out with anyone who's screaming," she yelled to him.

"You're going! We're going to celebrate your birthday."

She went into her bedroom and lay down on the bed. "Shit," she sighed. "It's going to be terrible."

"Look, it's no fun staying home with him in this state," I said. "And I'll be there."

Downstairs Buster sang along to songs he didn't know, interspersed with ear-shattering versions of "Happy Birthday to You." Or rather he howled.

In the car the perfume was at dangerously high levels, and my makeup was like the frosting on a cake.

"Well, you certainly look like a mature young lady," said my father from behind the wheel. But I felt more like a terrorist sitting near a bomb than a kid going out to celebrate.

This place was going to be a surprise, Buster assured us from behind the wheel. Different from what we were used to. Nan was quiet, so I started jabbering to fill the empty space. I told Buster about Gracie and her plans. He didn't acknowledge altruistic motives. I said that I believed, and so did Reich, that corporate reality was only one reality. He said to stop thinking so much, and he reminded me that it was his so-called corporate reality that paid for everything, including this evening out.

Now I sulked along with Nan.

Finally Buster parked the car outside a cheap-looking bar and restaurant called Manny's Hatcheck Room.

"What is this place?" asked Nan.

"It's not what it looks like," Buster promised us. "They got the greatest steaks in the city, and anyway, we don't have to stay long. Manny opens the show, and he's a funny guy."

He led us to the door. I went on alert. My father was tanked. Nan's face was drawn with worry and distrust.

"Who's the kid?" asked a beefy-looking man at the door. "She can't come in here."

"Hey, Tommy, she's no kid, she's my daughter," joked my father, and he slipped the guy a bill. Tommy shrugged and opened the door.

So that's why he wanted me to look older. I wasn't even legally supposed to be here. If I wasn't sure of that, I was positive the minute a nearly topless girl took our coats.

"I don't want to stay here," Nan said.

"Get inside." Buster was getting mean, but I hoped if we just listened to him it would pass.

Sitting around inside was a group of people I'd never come across. Guys who didn't have a complete set of teeth, but had plenty of tattoos, sat around drinking. They wore torn clothing and work boots and had grimy skin; the better off of them wore loud shirts and gold rings. The place was a raunchy dive. Sure, there was one table of preppy kids from Brooklyn College probably slumming after an exam or something. And there were a few men with their women, who all seemed to be dressed from Fredericks of Hollywood. But Buster had really gone off the deep end, I realized. How would Reich characterize this place, I wondered? Theories aside, I basically just wanted to evaporate.

Nan sat down at a table, acting as if by laying low and keeping silent she'd be out of the line of fire. She ordered a Perrier from a waitress wearing a flimsy blouse and tiny skirt. My father ordered vodka. I said I only wanted water. The waitress handed us oily menus.

"I want to leave," Nan whispered to Buster.

"*You* wanted to go *out*," he shouted malevolently. "Well, here we are, so let's have a *goddamn* good time."

That's when Manny arrived onstage wearing a toupee and lots of face makeup. He said he'd just arrived from Vegas. I wished he'd made a round trip.

"So this guy walks into a whorehouse," he began. On the word "whore," my mother rose out of her chair with the force of a small typhoon, but my father grabbed her wrist and forced her back down.

"Relax," he whispered. "Brogan's a big girl. You're okay, aren't you?" He looked at me. I shrugged unhappily.

"Yeah, so the guy asks for Molly O'Malley," continued Manny, "and the madam says, 'Are you kidding, Molly's booked up for six, oh, seven months in advance. She's the hottest number we got.' And the guy says, 'You tell Molly I got one thousand dollars right here in my hand to give her if she can see me today.' So the madam goes to check and sure enough she comes back and says, 'Okay, Molly will see you in an hour. Six sharp—be here.' And the guy comes back and sees Molly and they do it, and he gives her the money and makes a date for the next night. Same deal, same time, same money. And they do it again. He says 'Molly, you're such a lovely girl. I'm leaving town tomorrow, can I see you one more time?' She says, 'For the same dough, sure.' The last night is great, and he gives her another grand. She says, 'You seem like a nice guy. Where are you going back to?' 'Dublin,' he says. 'No kidding,' she says. 'My mother's from Dublin.' 'I know her!' says the guy. 'In fact, *she asked me to give you three thousand dollars!*' "

The audience clapped and pounded the tables.

I couldn't help but laugh, but I felt sick inside too. I wanted to jump inside a washing machine.

Seconds later I knew why. A mostly undressed woman slunk across the stage haughtily and without looking toward the audience. She was followed by another woman who suddenly threw off her slinky top and walked topless back and forth across the stage several times. This woman was probably forty, and she had bad skin and long hair teased for yards around her head. She was chewing gum the whole time, as if it weren't her who was really up there.

It was a strip joint! I was too dumbfounded to move.

My father leaned forward and signaled to the waitress to bring another round of drinks.

My mother got up, but her bag fell over and everything in it rolled out on the dirty wooden floor.

Another woman came onstage and lay down on an old couch. She took off her stockings, and bra with that self-same "who cares" attitude.

"Let's *go*!" I said. I bolted up and out through the smoke-filled, tacky room right into the ladies' room, where I heaved up everything in my stomach, hacking and coughing and crying all at once. The food flew out of me, and when I was done, I still gagged as if my insides could come up as well.

My mother flew into the bathroom and held my head. "I've got you," she said. "It's okay, just throw up and we'll get out of here." Finally I was done, and she gave me water, and made me gargle, and washed my face so I didn't feel disgusting. She had my coat with her and I put it on.

"Mom . . ." I said, without knowing how to finish the sentence. Though I must have felt disgust, disappointment, and betrayal, all I could actually think of was how strange the red-flecked velour of the bathroom walls looked, how cold my hands and feet were, and how very achingly tired I suddenly was.

We were out the front door in seconds, Nan waving wildly for a cab. Buster ran up to us as we hit the street, and that's when it really began. She slugged his arm with savage force. She cried and hit him, and unintelligible things spewed out of her mouth. The bowels of their marriage came out right there in front of Manny's Hatcheck Room, right where, I could imagine, other awful fights must have taken place. Buster backed away, growling at her, and the bouncer tried to usher them off to the side. But Nan kept at Buster, screaming bloodthirsty accusations until he finally untangled himself from her to scramble away to the car. He grabbed for my hand but Nan yanked me away. He peeled off from her invectives like a rocket.

Nan paced up and down the block, calling for a taxi, and I did the same. Eventually, one showed up. When we finally got home at midnight, Nan had to give the cabbie a check.

No Buster. Nan screamed to the walls that he had better not come back. What he was doing to her was one thing, but what he was doing to me was quite another. I thought of those awful conversations he'd had with me about mistresses.

Some birthday, Nan said. She wanted to kill him. So did I, but I told her to wait until morning. I fell into bed like a rescued child.

Chapter Eighteen

My glands secreted chemicals that made me go into a self-induced coma; I slept all day Sunday. Monday I woke up early and was the first person to get to school. When I got back home at four Nan informed me Buster wouldn't be coming home. Ever. Then around six he called and told me he'd see me Saturday and we would talk. His secretary got on to say how sorry she was. I grunted to both of them and hung up.

Nan and I were here together, alone. I was used to us being an unhappy threesome; I knew which way the currents blew, whom to side with, whom to avoid. I had no understanding of "two." And then there was Nan—I couldn't give her all the help she needed. What if she depended on me even more?

We sent out for Chinese food, which neither of us could make a dent in. Over hot and sour soup, she asked me how I felt. I told her I didn't know. She seemed disappointed. Maybe she wanted congratulations, or reassurance. Nan said she was doing the right thing—her breakthrough in pottery had given her back her soul, and the scene in the club had given her fight.

"Mom, what was the worst problem you had?"

She drew in breath like a tubercular person. "The worst problem was that we never should have married. Except to have you."

She smiled a sweet smile. It was fraught with feeling, a big fathoming of long-buried truths. I had forgotten that smile, but I was stung now by its power.

"We weren't suited. We knew it too for years, but there didn't seem to be anything to do about it. I got bogged down in the compromise. I shouldn't have but I did. That's how marriage is sometimes—"

"What else?"

She scrutinized me. "Brogan, you're old enough to hear this, I think. I knew your father was interested in other women. Frankly, I didn't care. I wasn't his lover—not for the last year." She sighed. "Here, try the pork fried rice."

So that explained the awful conversations and confidences Buster had had with me.

An impulse built: a frantic desire to see Mr. Price, tonight, soon, right after dinner. His face slammed against mine like a rushing ocean wave and made me giddy and frightened the way those waves did when they hit hard and pulled you under. I had to find out if he was really different from Buster. Did he really stand for everything he said in class?

Maybe he hadn't gotten involved with Rosanna, because, after all, wasn't real attraction in the brain? Rosanna wasn't his type mentally. I was. He cared about me in a different way, a much more profound way than about mere superficial looks. Mr. Price wasn't duplicitous or after cheap thrills. He was deep.

Or did I have it all wrong? Maybe Mr. Price was just like Buster, only with a different veneer. If he was, I could write off all men, couldn't I? I wanted to know tonight if I had to do that. It would be a big job and I would have to get started on it right away.

Nan would never let me leave the house, so I'd have to sneak out. I said good night, went upstairs, and made lots of noise brushing my teeth. I paraded in front of her in my nightgown, and made a big deal about saying good night again. Then I closed my door and began to drum up an outfit while I waited for her to go to bed. I kept having more and more time because she made several phone calls. I couldn't blame her—I wasn't much to talk to. But she was holding up my plan, and I'd already picked out black pants, low boots, a slinky turquoise blouse, long earrings, and plenty of mascara.

About eleven fifteen she took a shower. I padded downstairs, grabbed my jacket, and zoomed out the back door.

Before I left I'd looked at the street map. Unfortunately I'd have to walk, because Mr. Price didn't live near a bus or subway route. It took me nearly twenty cold and windy minutes, but I could have walked hours while the adrenaline pumped through me like expensive fuel. I had no idea what I would say to him when I got there. Or even if he'd be home. Or alone. And what if he weren't, what if Rosanna was there? I didn't care. I had to go no matter what I found.

If humans could explode simply by ringing buzzers, I would have been shredded like a shrapnel victim all over the carpet. His voice came through the intercom, asking who it was.

"Broganmyparentsaredivorcing." There was a minute's pause. "Please, I need to talk." He buzzed me in.

I hurried down long hallways with faded floral carpets. Pale, peeling paint shredded off the walls. But to me, walking to number 2J was as fascinating as being in the Louvre.

"Come in." Mr. Price had thrown on jeans and a gray sweatshirt. He looked tired but shatteringly handsome. The door to his bedroom was open and nobody else was there. I was finally alone with him, in his apartment.

I looked around. Two big brown velour sofas and lots of stereo equipment filled up the living room. There was a study in one corner, and framed Picasso posters.

"Tea, juice?" he asked, a little uncomfortable.

I shook my head no. I didn't want him to leave my sight.

"Brogan, are you okay? Sit down."

I sat. But no words came out.

He was patient. Still no words from me. I'd never seduced anyone before. I had to get him relaxed. Where to start? Talk about my mother and father? Me? Or school?

"My father drinks," I began. "No, that's not it," I said quickly. Somehow there was no flow of opinions now that I was standing in front of Mr. Price in his own home. I was dried up.

He just looked at me patiently.

"I hate to talk about it. It's ugly. And I have to take care of my mother because she falls apart. He gets mean to her."

"What else besides the drinking?"

"Last night he took us to a strip joint," I blurted out. Now, when I most wanted to be articulate, I was awkward, spluttering, hurting.

He shook his head.

"Didn't he know how it would make me feel? Worthless, like he was telling me I'm just a piece of meat like those other women. I'm *not* just a piece of meat."

"No, Brogan, you're a lovely girl."

"Lovely enough to kiss?" I tilted my head.

"Definitely."

Now *that* was a good answer! I waited but nothing happened. "Well . . ."

"Well what?" he said.

"Well, then why don't you?"

"Don't I what?"

"Kiss me!" I couldn't believe I had said it, but now I really wanted it to happen.

"Sorry, Brogan, I can't do that."

"Why not? Is it that I'm not sexy enough?"

"Brogan, don't be a jerk."

"Look, everyone knows what's going on with you and

Rosanna! So why not me? I need you more than she does. I'm better for you, anyway. I have substance and depth."

"Holy mackerel!" He jumped up and went to the kitchen to pour some water.

"Don't pretend you don't know what I'm talking about," I said in a threatening voice.

"Of course I know what you're talking about," he said from the sink.

My heart jammed. So it was true.

"I don't know where to begin," he said, sitting down.

"Do you love her?" I asked, my voice steady, like someone at a disaster site trying to remain calm.

"Brogan, Rosanna needed help. I can't go into the reasons, except to say she was becoming upset. And turning to bad things to make herself feel better."

"And you're a good thing to turn to, I bet. Well, I need help too. Didn't you hear what I told you?"

"And I'm trying to help you too."

"Good. Then kiss me." Then, as if I were possessed, I started opening my blouse. "I want you to *more* than kiss me."

He spilled the water when he leaped up from the couch.

"Button up, damn it," he shouted. "Nothing romantic, *nothing* sexual happened between Rosanna and me. Not even close. Yes, she had a crush on me, so I thought I could use my influence to help her. I'm not about to go into her family situation with you, Brogan—as I'm sure you would not like me to go around discussing yours with anyone— but I tried to help her in a critical time. Period. You think

I'd teach something like *The Greening of America,* then go fool around with my students?" He was mad.

I sat quietly, but my mind screamed. And spun. True, not true. Could I believe him? No, there was too much evidence. Did he think I was a fool?

Then he sat back down, without saying any more, and took my hand and stroked it. I became quiet. Maybe if I waited he'd get to kissing. Maybe we had to build the old-fashioned sexual tension. But he just kept stroking my hand. I squiggled closer to him. I wanted to feel his body. He put his arm around me and I thought I would go up in flames. Getting desperate, I said, "Don't you like me?"

"Like you! Of course I like you."

"Well, if you were allowed to . . . I mean if it was not against school policy or something, would you kiss me then?"

"Brogan, what you need now is a friend. You and that busy brain of yours."

But you don't kiss brains, I thought. You kiss beauty.

"If I were your age I'd be chasing you around the school, okay? Listen to me. You're unnerved now. You feel rejected. You're reaching out to me, and that's good, but sex isn't where it's at."

"It's not sex, it's love," I corrected him.

"Brogan, you are going to become someone terrific. You have a good and curious mind. You've made class challenging for me." He put his arm around me in a sort of avuncular way.

"Everybody believes there's a real thing going on between you and Rosanna," I said.

"Look, I'm thirty-four years old. I have my own life. I'm entrusted with an important job. I don't fall apart because I see a beautiful teenage girl."

"But you left Michelle's party with her."

"I took her to her home, where she cried for an hour. And I don't want to discuss her anymore. Now what about you?"

I sank into his chest. This place I'd wanted to be for so long. Then I jerked away. "Is this just professional kindness? I don't need professional kindness."

"You don't know what the hell you need." He pulled me back to him. "I could be asleep now. I could have not let you in. If I had only known . . ."

"Only known what?" Maybe now he would really open up and talk to me.

"If I had only known eight years ago what I was getting into when I decided to teach high school."

"How? How do you mean that?"

"I mean the torment some of you kids are in! You think it's easy to stand up there every day and see all that torment?"

"Well, I'd be in less torment if you would just kiss me. Once."

"You don't give up easily, do you? Well, basically that's a good character trait."

"Once?"

"Once and I'd break every responsibility entrusted to me."

"Is that what you told Rosanna?"

"As a matter of fact, yes! I'll tell you, I've learned something from all this. From now on, when I see trouble, I'm going to steer it to the lady in the guidance office. I'm not a god or a saint, a philosopher or a shrink, and I think I've learned that for once and for all. So I'm not bending any more rules—or going to any more parties.

"Now, let's talk about why you think you want to be involved with me. Do you have a boyfriend?"

"Boys my age are jerks."

"Some boys *my* age are jerks too." He laughed. I examined his eyes. All I could find was kindness.

"My parents got divorced when I was fourteen," he said quietly. "Divorce may be fashionable but it's never easy."

"So you're not going to kiss me? I was really counting on it."

"That's flattering."

He put an arm around me. Timidly at first, I leaned against him. I rubbed my face against his sweatshirt. I grabbed his chest with dockworker muscle. I needed to hold and be held.

I could never allow my father to hold me. It was impure, disquieting—his smells, his breathing, the hair on his face didn't offer protection. The very security I yearned for became, in his arms, dangerous to me.

But with Mr. Price, I found the very safety I'd given up hoping for. It soothed me, and for those moments in his arms, I had a home.

He rocked me. It took time for the trust to build and for the relief to spew out, but eventually they did, and my tears wet his sweatshirt and made it look like it had met up with a garden hose.

"Poor girl," he said, stroking my hair.

Light was filling the sky and the anarchic sounds of early-morning traffic began to replace the weary silence of night. Some time later a place of lightness began to grow inside me as well. I wouldn't have to write off all men, after all. I was relieved.

I used up the last tissue. In the soothing early-dawn air, the time of day that always seemed to promise so much, that seemed to be so perfectly innocent, Mr. Price held me beyond the point of necessity. He wasn't measuring.

I could taste the kindness and it tasted good.

Chapter Nineteen

I was trying to get off the phone with Michelle. She was asking me if I was going to talk to my father ever again, now that he was gone. As I'd already told her many times, I didn't really know. Some days she thought I should, especially when I told her my mother had heard that he'd quit drinking. Other days, she thought it was better that I didn't, because she saw how upset I became when she asked me about him. He called, of course, but I just froze and started seeing spots in front of my eyes.

Michelle and Art were back together, and Michelle was studying now and raising her hand in class. Mr. Price's class had awakened something in her, but when I told her Ira Moss said she had more than hairspray between her ears, and that she was getting less superficial by the minute, she said she was only trying to keep Art. "Less superficial is a permanent condition," I had answered. And it was true. She just kept going in class even though Art was devoted by now.

It was a month since Nan had decided to get serious about her work and to take on students. She even talked about having an exhibition.

And it was two weeks since Gracie had gotten enough afghan squares to make it across Flatbush Avenue, and her "Grandmas for Peace" got a photo in the newspaper.

My time was quiet. I was too filled up with my own experience to take in any more. Michelle and I were buddies again and really talking. But today she sounded like her old self. She wanted all the details about my date with Bruce Tailor, and I wasn't even dressed yet.

"I'll tell you everything *after*," I promised.

"I'm so glad he finally asked you out. You two are a perfect match!"

I didn't tell Michelle I had been flirting with Bruce lately. Slowly. Because I liked him. Because I knew it was the only time in my life I'd be a teenager and I didn't want to skip it just because of brain overdrive. "But why does it have to be roller-skating?" I moaned.

"It's a way to have *fun*," said Michelle, who pronounced "fun" like it had three syllables. "And that would make world history in any case."

"I know how to enjoy myself," I said defensively.

"You know about as much about having a good time as I know about molecular engineering," she said, "and

I failed biology last semester!" She hung up the phone.

I meant to tell her how I liked having her to talk to again. And I would, tomorrow. Now, I finished dressing.

She was right. Bruce and I matched in lots of ways: We were both thoughtful, involved with the Big Questions. Those Big Questions that would shape us whether we asked them or not, because who we are, what we stand for, what we believe, everything we do answers those questions. They work on us all the time, without our permission. Big Things were lying under every minute—ready to pounce, ready to become uncomfortable, ready to swallow us up. Things that hadn't been real yesterday. Bruce understood this.

When he came to the front door, wearing a cobalt-blue shirt that set off his eyes, a turbulence hit me like a summer storm. I stammered "hello" in a queer self-conscious way. Was it that he looked especially good, or that he was smiling broadly and confidently? I didn't know. Then I remembered how exquisitely he moved. Perhaps I felt a certain expectation rummaging around in my body.

"Hi! I hope I remember how to skate," I said finally.

"C'mon." He took my arm in his. "If you fail, you can make up a theory."

The rink was crowded, with the fast skaters zooming around the inside and the middle, and the slowpokes on the far outside. Bruce got on the floor, and his tall, elegant body zipped around with perfect ease. I loved the music and seeing the flow of humanity skate around with an almost weightless feeling. And Bruce. The passion I'd sensed smoldering inside him in class broke free when he used his body. He was transformed. I sensed indelibly that, like Bruce, we all have a greatness hidden in us somewhere, a gorgeous seed of something, and that the most important thing was to find it, dig it up, feed it, and help it to grow.

Suddenly I wanted to spin around. I wanted to turn, I wanted to speed and possibly fly.

"Don't wait for me," I urged Bruce, since I was actually skating with agonizing cautiousness, my hand grazing the edge of the rink for security.

He hesitated.

"Really, let me get warmed up."

He nodded and let his long legs carry him through the crowd. I lost him and concentrated on balancing and moving at the same time. It was just something I had to do, had to let my body do. I couldn't really think my way out of it, and that in itself was a relief. Then Bruce came up behind me and grabbed my waist, and slowly skated beside me. I fell into his rhythm, and a gurgle of pleasure let loose in my chest.

"A little faster," he said.

I kept up with him. He loosened his grip on me and then we just held hands.

"Eek!" I screamed around the first couple of curves. And then he let go of my hand and I was doing it alone. Sailing along. Free. Fast. Exhilarated. Letting the music pump me with drive. A smile broke out on my face with the simple pleasure of moving, of beating out gravity just a little bit. Gravity was a law you couldn't escape, but maybe there were times you had to play with it. Maybe that was something I could learn. Maybe I took gravity too personally. So I went faster still, zooming like some of the regular skaters and waving to Bruce, and for the first time in a long time I felt the innocence of my age. I wanted to feel more, so I pushed and pushed until I thought my skates would become wings and fly me right over the rink and up toward something truly wonderful.

Then there was a traffic jam and I couldn't move to the left or right—I hadn't really learned that yet. "Eek!" I screamed again. *"Eeekkkk!"*

I was down. Shocked. Laughing! Laughing so hard that when Bruce came to help me move to the side I couldn't even cooperate.

"You okay?" he kept asking.

"Yes, fine. I'm fine." Tears of hilarity wet my face. Falling down seemed so incredibly comic.

"No twisted ankles? Your bones are okay?" Bruce asked in absolute seriousness. He helped me up.

"My bones have never been better," I said. "Though my thigh is probably the color of chert by now." We were over by the side of the rink, heading toward the seats. Once I got up, I was a little shaken.

"Chert?"

We sat down. Bruce's face was flushed with concern.

"Chert is a geology term. Look," I asked, "how can I convince you I'm okay?"

"I don't know, Brogan. Please try."

He bent down to untie my shoes. His face grew very close. And in that instant I found myself giving Mr. Price back to the class, back to his own life; I let him go free, out of the strict enclosures of my mind. Bruce came closer still, close enough to kiss, and in another instant I gave magnificent-looking Rosanna back her beauty and knew I would not steal it again. Bruce's lips were so close to mine, and I knew I was going to swell with possibilities, drink my life in, and find my own way, and so kiss him I did. His lips tasted warm and sweet and a little urgent, and I was happy. And that was how I told him, and also myself, that I was okay, more than okay. I could say yes to my future.